PRAISE FOR AMANDA CROSS
AND
THE PLAYERS COME AGAIN

"If by some cruel oversight you haven't discovered Amanda Cross, you have an uncommon pleasure in store for you."
The New York Times Book Review

"Amanda Cross writes wonderfully witty mysteries full of well-developed characters and insights on modern foibles."
UPI

"Elegant and intelligent ... Another literate literary suspense story."
Raleigh News & Observer

"Cross is in top form here, writing the kind of witty, sophisticated story that will satisfy both fans of elegant mysteries and artful novels."
The Orlando Sentinel

THE PLAYERS COME AGAIN

Amanda Cross

BALLANTINE BOOKS • NEW YORK

Copyright © 1990 by Amanda Cross

All rights reserved under International and Pan-American Copyright Conventions. Published in the United States by Ballantine Books, a division of Random House, Inc., New York, and simultaneously in Canada by Random House of Canada Limited, Toronto.

Grateful acknowledgment is made to Viking Penguin, a division of Penguin Books USA Inc., for permission to reprint excerpts from "The Masks of Gods" from OCCIDENTAL MYTHOLOGY by Joseph Campbell. Copyright © 1964 by Joseph Campbell. Reprinted by permission of Viking Penguin, a division of Penguin Books USA Inc.

Library of Congress Catalog Card Number: 90-53122

ISBN 0-345-36998-X

This edition published by arrangement with Random House, Inc.

Manufactured in the United States of America

First Ballantine Books Edition: November 1991

To Grace K. Baruch

1936–1988

"The sweetness of this content overflowing runs down the walls of my mind, and liberates understanding. Wander no more, I say; this is the end. The oblong has been set upon the square; the spiral is on top. We have been hauled over the shingle, down to the sea. The players come again."

—VIRGINIA WOOLF,
The Waves

Part One

One

LATE that year as the eighties were beginning to run out, with Christmas and the end of the semester looming, Kate Fansler found herself at a loose end. Her study of Henry James and Thomas Hardy, which had taken far too long to write, as academic books always did, had finally been published to general approbation and the usual snappy remarks about American scholarship that passed for a review in the *Times Literary Supplement*. Kate had spent about four months in a state of abject relief, cleaning up her desk and trying to make amends for the many old letters long unanswered and the new letters inspired by the appearance of her book. This fallow period had its advantages, but it was beginning to pall. Into this vacuum crept the insidious realization that she never again wished to publish a work of literary criticism. Unfortunately she did not, on the other hand, wish to "look into her heart and write," as the poet's muse had instructed him. Many women and men she knew had abandoned criticism for examinations of their personal lives and experience, and while she compulsively read the products of their internal examinations with interest and occasionally startled recognition, she had no desire or inclination to go and do likewise. Excluded alike from literary studies and memoirs, she wondered if another project would ever occur to her.

Into this desert of intention there intruded an editor from one of the six biggest publishing houses dominating the book world. They were all owned and, one understood, directed as to the bottom line by vast organizations whose principle product was oil, or motor cars, or widgets. Kate had so far had nothing whatever to do with them.

The editor's name was Simon Pearlstine, and he had astonished Kate by inviting her to a very expensive and extended lunch, a remarkable act from one whom she had never met or heard of. But he, it soon transpired, had heard of her.

"From many people," he assured her as they were shown to their table. "You have quite a reputation among scholars. Won't you have a drink? I can't drink at lunch anymore, but you must, please."

"You," Kate said, "will have soda water and lime, a lettuce leaf, and decaffeinated coffee. I will have a vodka martini on the rocks with lemon peel, and whatever the waiter most heartily recommends." It turned out that not the waiter but someone further along in the hierarchy took their order, and was delighted to recommend what he assured Kate would be a masterpiece of a lunch. She acquiesced in her most ladylike manner. Doubtless Mr. Pearlstine wanted something, and she was prepared to enjoy herself while discovering what it was. She requested, and was granted, a Beaune wine with her main course, and settled happily back to listen and, she was certain, refuse.

Simon Pearlstine seemed ready to circle around the point of this lunch as she sipped her exquisite martini.

"What do you know about Emmanuel Foxx?" he asked.

"What everyone knows; perhaps a trifle more, given my profession," she answered, wondering why he was playing at twenty questions; well, it was his invitation and his expense account. "I do teach the British novel," she added, by way of explaining her immodest claim.

"And what do you think of him?"

"Meaning what?" Kate asked, considering another martini and deciding that she would wait for the Beaune. "He is a novelist of the first rank, as we say when a writer has accumulated a madly impressive body of criticism. He is one of the major figures of high modernism. He is right up there with Joyce and Lawrence and Woolf and Conrad, perhaps more influential in the long run than any but Joyce and Woolf. Two decades ago I would have said Conrad and Lawrence, but no longer. How extended a lecture did you require?" She smiled at him, to take away the sting of her question.

"Do you personally like him?"

"Do I curl up with him on long winter evenings? No. My greatest affection, as my last book might suggest [she wondered if he had read it, and referred to it with some self-consciousness] is for a slightly earlier time. I also suspect," she added, letting the martini induce abandon, "that he rather overestimated the amount of energy women expend on sex. But that may be more a function of my age than his verisimilitude."

"May I call you Kate?" Pearlstine asked, having considered her remark. Kate nodded. "I'm glad you said that," he continued, "because I think you are probably right. One of the defenses of the veracity of his portrait, you know, is that the protagonist is based on his wife. Some even think she helped him to write *Ariadne*, though that opinion's rather recent."

"I've heard it," Kate said.

"And you believe it?"

"I don't think so. It's an intriguing possibility, but there is little evidence. I mean, if you read *The Autobiography of Alice B. Toklas,* which Gertrude Stein wrote, and then read some of Alice Toklas's own works written after Stein's death, you might argue that the style of *The Autobiography* resembles Toklas more than Stein. I'm not saying, you understand, that Toklas wrote it, and my knowledge of American literature is close to feeble anyway. I'm just suggesting that there's some outside evidence of how Toklas wrote."

Had Simon Pearlstine known Kate better he would have understood, indeed he may have guessed if he was a man of sharp perceptions, that she was talking in her wandering mode, a habit she had long since developed for saying nothing while seeming friendly and responsive, rather as a Shakespearean actor in repertory keeps on with his speech till he remembers what play he's in. Kate wondered when Simon Pearlstine would come to the point, or even if he had one.

"I see what you mean," he said now, "and it is an opinion of great significance in the light of what I want you to do." Here they were interrupted by the waiter with their lunch, and the ceremonial opening of Kate's wine bottle.

The waiter offered her some to taste, and she did so with evident delight.

"Hadn't you better let it breathe?" Simon asked.

"The rest of the bottle can breathe along with me," Kate said, smiling. "Don't you think you'd better tell me what you want from me that is worth this elegant wine?"

"I want you to write a biography of Gabrielle Foxx."

Kate choked on her wine, which was sacrilege and a terrible waste. She began coughing, and found it difficult to stop.

"Do I do the Heimlich maneuver?" Pearlstine asked. The waiter and the maître d' had also rushed over.

"I'll be all right in a moment," Kate said, coughing away. "Just ignore me if you can." She sipped water and with increasing success tried to breathe naturally.

"Sorry," Pearlstine said when the fit seemed over. "I hope your reasoned response will not be so violent—unless, of course, it's positive."

"I've never written a biography."

"I know that. But you used biographical material with a most enviable delicacy in your book on James and Hardy. And I thought you might be in a mood to consider a different sort of challenge." He paused, but didn't seem to want Kate to speak just yet. "Every book on Foxx speaks of her as an aspect of him, a major event in his life. I think it's time she was the subject of her own story. And if you add the fact that his famous protagonist is a woman, you seem to me to have a very strong argument for a biography. We are prepared," he added, in an offhand manner as he returned to his salad, "to offer a handsome advance. Very handsome."

Kate was about to speak, but again he stopped her.

"Don't answer now. Eat your specially recommended lunch; drink your wine. Let's talk about cabbages and kings. Let's arrange to meet in exactly two weeks, same time, same station, and talk about it further. Try to keep from deciding upon a definite no until after your second lunch. May I ask that of you?"

For the first time Kate looked at Pearlstine seriously. She had had him neatly pigeonholed: editor, persuader, and, as were all those in publishing these days, master salesman. But something about him seemed to whisper of more than that. Kate considered an intelligent editor to be almost as rare as a patient doctor and, therefore, equally welcome even if, at the moment, one had no pressing need for either.

"I'll think about it," she said. "But aren't there many biographies of Foxx himself that have scoured the sources for material on Gabrielle? I know biographies must be constantly rewritten, but surely biographers don't actually ignore material or make things up where documentation is available."

"True. There hasn't been a Foxx biography since Mark Hansford's, and that was mainly notable for the new pictures he dug up, I understand from someone in the Goddard family. Foxx's son married a Hilda Goddard. I think a woman doing Gabrielle's biography would be likely to have new insights; anyway, I admire your work and would like to publish something by you. Think about it, that's all I ask."

"I can certainly agree to that," Kate said. Simon Pearlstine reached under the table, and magicianlike, produced a copy of the Hansford biography. Kate took it, placing it on her side of the table, and sipped her Beaune to emphasize her promise to reread Hansford and think about a life of Gabrielle. It is a distinct tribute to the elegance of Beaune wine that the idea did not seem absolutely and finally impossible.

Having enjoyed her lunch and wine and having, in that enjoyment, sacrificed an afternoon of work, Kate went off to a much-touted exhibition at the Metropolitan and listened on her audio enabler (or whatever it was called) to the mellifluous tones of the curator of painting (or whatever he was) at that exalted institution.

It was therefore considerably later in the evening when Kate finally settled down with Mark Hansford's biography of Emmanuel Foxx. The edition Pearlstine had given her was a new one to mark the tenth anniversary of the biography's original publication. A new preface for this edition by the author mentioned that he had originally missed the twenty-fifth anniversary of the publication of *Ariadne* by a year, but that he had been enabled to publish his biography only a year later thanks to Dorinda Goddard Nicholson, to whom he had dedicated the original edition of his biography, and whose kindness and generosity had allowed him to finish his biography quickly and, he believed, well. Dorinda Goddard Nicholson, he explained, was the niece of the woman who had married Emmanuel Foxx's son and the heir of many pictures of the Foxx family. This new, anniversary edition of his biography, while in no way less indebted to the generosity of Dorinda Goddard Nicholson, he would like to dedicate to his wife, Judith. The new preface was followed by a list of illustrations, and indeed these were the heart of the book. Each of them was from the collection of Dorinda Goddard Nicholson or photographed by her, except for a few that had been lent by someone named Anne Gringold, who had herself taken photographs of members of the Foxx family in past years. Kate found the names and connections confusing, but decided to postpone that puzzle for later contemplation.

The pictures were indeed wonderful, and almost all of them published for the first time. Chief among these was a stunning 1926 portrait of Emmanuel Foxx, taken by a renowned photographer of the period who had been paid by Sig Goddard, Dorinda's father. By this time Foxx was of course famous and had been frequently photographed, but this particular picture had a unique quality of perception rare even in brilliant painted portraits by great artists. Hansford explained that it had not previously been published because Foxx had not liked it, so all copies not destroyed by him were in the possession of Sig Goddard, who had paid the bill. Kate wondered what had persuaded the Goddards to cough it up at this particular moment; perhaps it had only recently been discovered in some cupboard. Kate could see why Foxx had disliked it. It had been taken shortly before the publication of *Ariadne* when Foxx's reputation was high, but not as high as it would be after the publication of that masterpiece. Chapters of the novel had already appeared in some avant-garde publications, and expectations for its publication as a whole were at their height.

Foxx, his familiar leonine head (indeed his hair resembled nothing so much as a mane) flung back as he sat, one leg crossed over the other and his hands clasped like a fighter's in a pose of self-congratulation, in a chair which, with its high back and squared-off arms, oddly resembled a throne, had a look of profound self-satisfaction. It was a look one might imagine on the face of Mephistopheles after striking the bargain with Faust. Seen in retrospect, once one knew of the great literary accomplishment lying only a year in the future, the portrait hardly seemed in its pose of grandeur to claim too much. Foxx was now dead about fifty years, and that he had known or guessed at his immortality as a great writer and refused any becoming modesty in contemplation of that reputation seemed only to add to his accomplishment. But at the time the photograph must have been seen as claiming too much, too soon. Other pictures taken then by the same photographer were, at the time of Hansford's biography, famous: he had reproduced only one of them. It was a picture of Gabrielle standing awkwardly at a window out of which she stared as though eager to ignore the photographer.

Kate studied Gabrielle's face; her photograph was placed in Hansford's book across from the picture of Emmanuel Foxx: each portrait occupied a whole page, and acquired, in contrast, a startling effect. Foxx faced the camera's gaze in triumph; she avoided it in shame. Or was this only Kate's fancy? Kate had once gone to speak at a woman's college in a large room furnished like a grand parlor but capable of holding rows of folding chairs. On one wall hung two large portraits of the man who had given the money for the room—it bore his name—and his wife, who had herself attended the college. During the announcements preceding her talks and the somewhat extended introduction of herself, Kate had gazed fascinated at the pictures. The man declared himself to the world, staring forth, if not in arrogance, certainly with astonishing assurance. But the woman was merely looked at. She had on her best dress, her pearls, her hair had been carefully arranged. But she seemed simultaneously to allow herself to be stared at and to deny its necessity. He looked, she was looked at, that was what it amounted to.

Gabrielle had refused to admit she was being contemplated. She had looked away from the camera toward some place outside the scene being photographed. The photographer, perhaps not content with only a profile of her, had caught three quarters of the averted face, caught in addition the reflection of her face in the window so that if she appeared to acknowledge anything in that room, it was herself.

The photographs in Hansford's book had been divided into two sections: the first, early in the book, comprised the by now familiar pictures of Foxx when young, Gabrielle when young, and places in England where they had spent their youths; the second section, twice as large, was of pictures provided by Dorinda Goddard Nicholson, most of them new, all of them clearly the strong selling point for this otherwise unmemorable biography of which Kate, at any rate, remembered few if any revelations from her first reading.

The Goddard pictures, as Kate thought of them, the ones here published for the first time, were not only of Emmanuel Foxx but also of his wife, Gabrielle, his son, Emile, his daughter-in-law, Hilda; there was also a picture of Dorinda herself, Anne Gringold (whose connection with Dorinda Kate could hardly fathom), and Nellie, Emmanuel Foxx's granddaughter, taken after she had arrived in the United States. The mysterious Anne Gringold had provided a picture of the house in which Gabrielle had lived in London in the 1950s, and Nellie had taken a picture of Gabrielle a few years earlier, long after Emmanuel Foxx's death and before she had moved to London. In this picture Gabrielle had aged, but she looked straight at the camera, as though to say "Yes, look at me, I am here." There was also a picture of

Gabrielle and Nellie together, apparently taken by Nellie with one of those self-timers that can be set, allowing the photographer to hurl herself, grinning with triumph, into the picture just before the click of the shutter. Both of these pictures had apparently been sent to Dorinda and subsequently lent by her to Mark Hansford.

Was there any reason to suppose a biography of Gabrielle would be of genuine interest, or serve as more than a footnote to the life and works of a modern master? Biographies of women were, in the last decades, greatly in demand by readers and publishers alike, but was that sufficient reason to increase their number, or at least to persuade Kate to do so? She stared for a time at the complementary portraits of Foxx and Gabrielle, and then settled down to reread the book from the beginning.

Simon Pearlstine had been clever to offer it to her, given his hopes, for the book fairly cried out for more about Gabrielle. Where, Hansford seemed constantly to ask, had Foxx got his knowledge of female emotion and desire? Had he not turned to Gabrielle for help, advice, perhaps even for actual written descriptions? Hansford referred, not very obliquely, to the way in which Colette's husband had locked her in a room and forced her to write out the accounts of her school days, including her sexual adventures, explorations, and experiments. Other men had attempted to portray a woman's psyche: Lawrence certainly, and Joyce of course in the uncorseted and, for their time, shocking thoughts of Molly Bloom as she lay in bed, menstruated, masturbated, recalled her conquests, and assiduously avoided (as women do when thinking?) all punctuation and established syntax. True, Dorothy Richardson had done something of the sort: written the thoughts of a woman in a form that the male establishment had found hardly enticing, and of which Graham Greene had complained that the dreary Miriam had finally lost her virginity on page four hundred and something, perhaps to his mind her most notable achievement, a judgment with which Hansford appeared to agree and to which Kate emphatically objected. But Emmanuel Foxx had certainly outdone them all: devoted an entire book, linguistically revolutionary, exquisitely crafted, to the life and thoughts and passions of a woman. He had guessed, Hansford declared, that man's fascination and obsession with woman, as well as his terror of her newly empowered voice, desires, and ambitions, would reveal themselves as to the very heart of modernism. And so, in time, they had. But what had Gabrielle to do with all this, besides bearing his child, loving him, and giving him her life? Did she prepare more than his food and his laundry? That was the haunting question, Hansford declared.

Well, Kate asked herself, did she? The book was not long; even perhaps in intent if not in size, a coffee-table book. It had been cleverly stretched out to disguise the sparsity of text. Kate, reading into the night, was able to finish it. All the old facts were there, the old facts and the new question about Gabrielle's part in the creation of *Ariadne*.

But was there any real reason to ask it? The only answer was, in its turn, another question: how had Gabrielle lived her life, and what, besides her love for Emmanuel Foxx, had kept her going? She must have been aware (Hansford said as much) that she was considered an appendage to her husband, a necessary but regrettable part of his life and work. Dorinda Goddard Nicholson had told Hansford that

Hilda had not spoken much of Gabrielle, nor had her husband, Gabrielle's son, Emile.

One knew in the end remarkably little about Gabrielle. Or did one? Perhaps Hansford, like earlier biographers, had simply not searched with sufficient rigor. Kate bethought herself, laughing, of John le Carré, in whose books she delighted. Now, if one could only get John le Carré's British secret service to do the groundwork for a biography. In five days, they could discover all there was to know about a person's past, present, and likely future: they tapped telephones, undertook interviews on phony excuses, learned all a person's haunts, habits, what and where they drank, ate, made love, hung out, and worked. Of course, the subject of the secret service's remarkable endeavors was alive and in a position to spy for England. Still, they resurrected the past with an efficiency any biographer might envy. Was it only the secret service that had the money and the employees to undertake such horrible probing? Many said J. Edgar Hoover had turned these investigative powers onto Martin Luther King and others he thought dangerous to America's ideas of white supremacy and anticommunism. Kate had read somewhere that tapping telephones was child's play in the current world; England's were tapped by the government as a matter of course, she had been informed. But, what had this to do with poor Gabrielle?

Kate, my dear, she said to herself, you are wandering off into your detective mode. But wasn't that the point of remembering le Carré? No, it wasn't. The point was that detectives are not biographers, and secret services least of all. In fact, as she thought about it, the point of le Carré's excellent books was precisely that the more you knew people, the less you knew them. Tapping telephones, in the end, might give you information, but it did not give you understanding. Kate smiled. Thanks be for the unpredictabilities of human nature. It was not that the likes of Hoover and the British secret service lacked for answers; what they lacked were the right questions.

Which a biographer might ask? Which she, Kate Fansler, might ask? Kate had a totally indefensible belief in destiny, providence, the wisdom of chance. Such a belief could scarcely be expressed, let alone defended. But wasn't Simon Pearlstine's offer just the sort of opportunity that earlier, simpler times and people attributed to divine benevolence? No, she could have no part of divine benevolence; yet opportunities lost, tides not taken on the rise, chances declined, could certainly add up to a life lived rather drearily on one track and in the path of safety and sullen self-satisfaction. Wasn't that, after all, why her vocation of amateur detective had been so appealing? Had she ever sought a case in her life? No, she had not. They had come to her, and she had pursued them because when you are called you must answer, or, as with some of le Carré's heroes, adamantly refuse. But you could not wobble in indecision and laxity. End of lecture.

All of Kate's "cases" had called upon, if not exactly needed, her literary skills honed in the world of academic criticism and scholarship. She attracted those cases which called for her particular talents, or which seemed to. That was why she was not, all other more obvious reasons apart, a private investigator rather than a professor of literature. One could hardly hang out a shingle inviting only those cases with literary ramifications.

Gabrielle Foxx. What had her maiden name been? Kate consulted the index of Hansford's book: Howard. Gabrielle

Howard Foxx. Born 1889; ran off to Paris with Emmanuel, 1905. Only child, Emile, born 1906. Emile married to Hilda in 1925. Grandchild Nellie born 1926. Emmanuel died in 1942. Emile presumed dead, 1944. Gabrielle moved back to England in 1950. Died in 1959.

Kate listed these dates, extracted with some difficulty from Hansford's biography: he had not provided a chronology except of Foxx's publications. Did these dates constitute a life? They would have long been thought properly to constitute a female life, certainly in the days when a woman's name was printed in the newspapers at her birth, marriage, death, and never else. Why was Gabrielle even possible as the subject of a biography? Because she had run off with and lived with and perhaps inspired a famous writer, one of the pillars of high modernism?

Kate turned back to the picture, to the face looking out the window, away from the figure in the thronelike chair. Well, suppose one of those Goddards or Nellie Foxx had hired her to find out all there was to be found out about Gabrielle? Would she take it as a case? Probably. Would she take it as a literary enterprise encompassing the work of many years? That was less likely.

Which was where, in fact, Kate's thoughts remained for one of the two weeks before her next meeting with Simon Pearlstine.

At the start of the second week, when the whole idea of a biography of Gabrielle had receded to the back of Kate's mind and, she was inclined to believe, the realm of the unlikely, she received an envelope from Simon Pearlstine, delivered by messenger. It was a large brown envelope, containing a short manuscript and a covering letter. Pearlstine had written:

Dear Kate (if I may):

Whether or not you agree to do the biography of Gabrielle—and of course I hope and pray that you will agree—I have decided to trust you with the enclosed. It is a most intriguing (I find) account by Anne Gringold of her life with the Goddards. She was, as you will discover, also about the last person to see Gabrielle in her proper self, before her stroke or whatever it was.

I shall save for our next meeting (same time, same place one week hence) an explanation of how this came into my hands. Anne needed money, that is the long and short of it, and gave it to someone who trusted me to deal fairly with it. And so I trust you with it now. I hope, of course, that it will entice you to undertake the biography. If these pages and I fail, I know I can trust you to keep their contents secret and to return them to me without showing them to anyone else. You see what confidence I have in you.

Until next week,
Simon

Typed by himself.

Kate turned to the enclosed manuscript, glancing at its first phrase: " 'He is the greatest writer of his time,' Dorinda said . . ." She read through to the end without stopping.

Simon was waiting for Kate when she arrived. "A vodka martini?" he asked.

"Not today," Kate said. "Today I'm with you all the way, designer water, salad, coffee—not decaffeinated, so I guess it's not all the way. Some things I can't give up, even for Gabrielle."

"I trust that's a good sign," Simon said, before giving the order to the waiter.

"Well, if I give up the Beaune, it probably is," Kate said. "But in fact, I drink only at frivolous lunches, and at all dinners. How did you come upon that Anne Gringold manuscript?"

"A friend of a friend of a friend. Hush, hush, of course. Except to say that Anne needed money, this was her most salable item, but she wanted it to fall only into good hands: those you see before me."

"And that's what inspired you to ask me to do the biography?"

"I should have been inspired to ask you in any case; you came to me as an inspiration all on your own. But I do admit to hoping that Anne's tale would swing the odds in my favor."

"You paid her for it, adequately, generously?"

"Yes, my dear Kate Fansler, I did. And offered her a further fee if it were used in a biography. If it isn't used, she'll be free to sell it on the open market. Meanwhile I offered and she gratefully received a handsome price, handsome I do assure you."

"In the same class of handsome as my proposed advance."

"A woman of perspicacity."

"You do realize that I have never written a book for what I believe is called the trade market? All my scholarly and critical endeavors have been published by university presses. Are you sure I shall be readable enough to sell?"

"All my editorial instincts point to that conclusion."

19

"Exciting as Anne Gringold's account is, it tells us relatively little about Gabrielle. Only that she has Gabrielle's papers. One must assume, if she has agreed to publication, that she wants someone to pursue them. But if found, won't they in fact belong to Nellie as Gabrielle's heir?"

"No. I was able to determine that. After all, I don't want a lawsuit on our hands. Gabrielle made out a codicil to her will just before Anne came to see her. It left her papers absolutely to Anne Gringold, stating only that in the event that they were ever sold for a sum of money, half of that sum would go to Nellie or her heirs, the other half to remain with Anne."

"It certainly does arouse one's detective instincts."

"So I hoped; a detective and a scholar, to say nothing of a published author of remarkably readable prose. Dare I hope, dare I suspect, Kate Fansler, that you are caught? That I may draw up a contract?"

"I don't even have an agent."

"You don't need one. But lest you think I am trying to pull the wool over your eyes, let me hasten to say that I suggest you show the contract to your lawyer husband. If he doesn't feel competent in publishing matters, he must know someone who does."

"Are you trying to make me say yes at this very moment?"

"I am, I am. Shall we each have a vodka martini?"

"Make it a half-bottle of Beaune."

Simon signaled to the waiter and gave the order. They sat in silence while the wine steward fetched the bottle, ordered the glasses, poured out the first taste.

"We'll both taste it," Simon said. And he held up his glass with only a bit of the crimson magic in the bottom.

''To Gabrielle,'' he said.

''Or,'' Kate responded, raising her glass in turn, ''to this ship and all who sail in her, as John le Carré would say.''

''Maybe I should have tried to get him to write the biography,'' Simon said, laughing.

''Too late; you've got me,'' Kate Fansler said.

Part Two

Two

"HE is the greatest writer of his time," Dorinda said, in that tone children use when quoting established parental opinion. "Perhaps," she added, "of any time. And he is a relation of ours."

"By marriage," I pointed out. This was not particularly generous of me. Dorinda had been so endowed by life with all the elements of charm and wealth that her claim to the greatest writer seemed, at the least, to be gilding the lily. (This last was a phrase of my mother's whose meaning I had discerned through use rather than analysis of its metaphor or knowledge of its source.)

"His grandchild is certainly our relation," Dorinda said, closing, as was her invariable habit, the discussion. Since the great writer's son had married Dorinda's father's sister, no argument was possible. An only child like me, she now had a cousin her age with a romantic and war-torn past, due to appear out of the blue (of the ocean, not the sky) and add to Dorinda's life more romance, a commodity of which, in my opinion, she already had an unfair share. The only overwhelming disappointment, which loyalty to my sex forbade my pointing out even though it might have punctured a little Dorinda's boasts, was that the grandchild was a girl. A boy, in this case as, I was certain, in all cases, was what had been longed for. Still, this girl bore the magic name and might even, like Margaret Mead, a hero of mine, decline to change it upon marriage or, even more daringly, decline to marry. At that point, the car drove up, the chauffeur honked and we rushed out to be driven to the beach club and our ocean games.

This memory, from the time just before America entered into World War II, returns to me like a flashback from the sort of movie they used to make when I was young. Except that those flashbacks were extended, and full of portent. My memories, which have seized me more often and more unexpectedly in recent years, are like a photograph flashed on the wall. I was an ardent photographer in those young days and for many years thereafter. I had an excellent camera, thanks again to Dorinda and her family, and Dorinda had taught me how to flash pictures, not yet in color, on the wall through a large projector. I see us, therefore, sitting on the huge porch of her summer home on the Jersey shore, swinging our rockers violently backward, awaiting our ride to the beach. The conversation is not in the picture, not even (in my memory) in balloons above our heads, as though we were cartoon figures. Rather, the language *is* the scene; is what the scene evokes, is that remembered moment. A movie from a later time, called *Hiroshima, Mon Amour*, was, in my opinion, the last to capture memory properly. Movies today are all crosscuts and violent effects, screams, movements. Memories (as opposed to traumas, or repressed scenes) are still; only the words speak. But, in my experience at least, they are always insignificant memories that have remained for no discernible reason, ready to be evoked by a chance occurrence or remark. (Once, when Dorinda and I were in the car with her parents, the chauffeur driving, Dorinda and I on the jump seats, a fly buzzed about us in the summer heat. "And I thought," Dorinda told me later, "that I would never remember that fly and, of course having said that, will always remember it." I never thought to ask her when we met again, both well into middle age, if she had remembered it. But I remembered for her, after all.)

The year when Dorinda's cousin arrived was 1941. We would all three be together at the end of that year, when Pearl Harbor was bombed. I remember that we were in Dorinda's room, and her mother, who had been listening to the Philharmonic concert on the radio, came in to tell us the concert had been interrupted with the news. Every adult I knew at that time, if home on Sunday, listened to the Philharmonic: my mother, my aunts, the parents of my and Dorinda's schoolmates. Such concerts seemed to me oddly appropriate as the channel for the news that we were at war. Dorinda, her cousin Nellie, and I settled into the life of wartime America. We all rejoiced that Nellie had been plucked from the disaster that was Europe. I knew of others similarly plucked, who turned up as guests in the elegant homes where my mother worked. But they were different,

27

part of my secret life with my mother, resented, overtly scorned and snubbed.

"Why do they criticize everything here," I asked my mother. "Why aren't they grateful? Why do they always talk about how much better everything was in Germany? If it was so much better, why didn't they stay there?"

I did not then know mine was a widespread and stupid question; what immigrant or refugee does not think of home? I suspect I hated them because they were Jews and allowed me the regrettable comfort a poor child might find in Jew-hating. It was altogether a different matter for Dorinda, whose family, an integral part of what came to be known as "Our Crowd," were friends with Guggenheims and Warburgs, to be Jewish. They were as elegant as Episcopalians and almost indistinguishable. Besides, Dorinda's mother was a gentile who used to take us to midnight mass at her Lutheran church. I forgave myself my anti-Semitism by the ridiculous canard that some of my best friends were Jews. My mother supported me in this neat and, as it turned out, universal dismissal of the Jewish question. She said that nobody bothered honorable people; I suppose she meant rich. Years later, when I read a book by Paule Marshall called *Brown Girl, Brownstones* in which she talks of her mother's cleaning "Jew floors," I felt ashamed, and with less excuse than Paule Marshall had. She was black, and had not known Dorinda and her family.

The greatest writer of his time was named Foxx; Emmanuel Foxx. I did not remember having heard of him when Dorinda broke the news of his granddaughter's coming; but my mother had a first edition of his most famous novel among her books when she died, and she had written in it the date of its acquisition; she must at least have mentioned him to me at an earlier time. I suspect that, as with many declared masterpieces, his novel was ardently read by scholars and skimmed or ignored by those intelligent ones, few enough in every country, who, uninstructed, read books constantly and eagerly. Unlike Virginia Woolf, but like James Joyce or Marcel Proust, he was more an academic's than a reader's passion. Perhaps he was nearer to Proust than Joyce. Certainly he stood, as I now understand, together with these two and T. S. Eliot, at the center of modernism as it was conceived in academic departments and learned books and articles. Unlike Joyce or Proust, however, his central character was a woman. With an intensity, attention to detail, and experimentation with language that was dumbfounding in its originality and inventiveness, Foxx had written a year in the life of a woman that followed, with dogged persistence and great ingenuity, her every thought and passion. She was a woman seen through the eyes of a man looking through her eyes, and she set the scholars many a profound challenge.

All of this, of course, I learned later. In 1941, awaiting Nellie Foxx's arrival, I knew only that her grandfather had written an impressive and in some ways obscene book whose publication had been won by the efforts of the enlightened—including Dorinda's father—against the benighted, the protectors of public morals. Foxx's female hero masturbated, menstruated, fantasized, but was forever distinguished from Joyce's Molly Bloom by her high intelligence, her allegiance to her women friends, her ambivalence toward men, whom she admired, emulated, and despised, and her sexual attraction to women. It was a scene of lesbian lovemaking that had got the book banned, although in 1941 Dorinda and I did not know that, Dorinda claiming to be an expert only in heterosexual cavortings. Young people today find it hard to believe, but we did not even know the word *lesbian*, nor the possibility of such activity. Like Queen Victoria, we thought only men had the equipment or the nerve for sexual experimentation; we had of course heard of male homosexuals and referred to them, sneeringly, as "fairies" or "thataway." We were the children of our time.

What I chiefly recall (as opposed to having flashed before me as a memory) is the amazing generosity of Dorinda and her family. Dorinda had adopted me as bosom friend, and her parents allowed me to be her almost constant companion. For example, when Dorinda was given something, I was given something too. As with cameras: in order to help out some German refugees, Dorinda's father bought cameras from them, Leica M3s, and he gave the best one to Dorinda, and another, for some reason inferior, to me. We became photographers, good photographers, and even years later, when single-lens reflex cameras were almost universal, I stuck to my old Leica with its range finder and its heavy metal case. I have it yet, and when I take it for some repair, I am told it will fetch a handsome price if I ever decide to sell it and join the contemporary camera world. I keep it, not from sentiment, but from admiration. It is, in my opinion, the best camera ever made.

But it was not alone in such generous gifts that the Goddards expressed themselves. They made me part of their family, without ever making me feel like a poor relation. The maid who picked up and washed Dorinda's dirty clothes would seek mine in my suitcase where I had hoped to conceal them: in a short time they were returned to me, cleaned and ironed. The maids never treated me in any way as an inferior, and I know now that Dorinda's mother must have assured this by giving them extra money and talking to them. My mother spoke sometimes of whether or not I ought to tip the maids as a guest in the house, but nothing ever came of this. We decided that a child would not have been expected to hand money to a servant.

I feared horribly that the arrival of Nellie would signal my expulsion from this paradise. Nellie would become the substitute companion, and I would gradually be dropped. My mother had been troubled by my friendship with people as rich and elevated as Dorinda's family, and now, with Nellie's coming, she warned me I would suffer what she had always feared: the betrayal of my trust and the discomfort of my return to the life she was able to offer me, a life not only ordinary but tense and threatened.

The miracle is that this never happened, that we continued as three, that Dorinda never, until many years later at least, felt anything but loyalty to us both. And since she had the money, and we did not, we all shared in it. Dorinda told us she was practicing socialism on a small scale; no doubt she was closer to what in later years would be called, with a sneer, a Lady Bountiful, but I can testify that her benevolence, involving no evident privileged class and no bureaucracy, seemed simply ideal.

My mother worked as a housekeeper in the various homes of the very rich. I had met Dorinda because my mother had been lent by a New Jersey neighbor to Dorinda's mother during a summer week. In those days, the coast of New Jersey was known as the Jewish Newport; I have recently read in an autobiography by Peggy Guggenheim that she despised it: the huge houses, the many servants, the roses and hydrangeas which alone would grow in that climate. I came upon the Peggy Guggenheim book quite by accident not too long ago, and it brought back to me those heavenly summers; only to a Guggenheim could they have seemed tacky. To me, they were the good life, and whenever the good life was invoked, whether of Cole Porter on the Riviera or the Kennedys in Hyannisport, the picture of that life, even in my mature and worldly mind, was New Jersey in the years before and during World War II.

I suppose I seemed a challenge to Dorinda when we met; we were twelve years old. My mother had got permission to bring me with her to Dorinda's house; I was the perfect child of an upper servant—quiet, unobtrusive, observant, full of longing. But Dorinda, who was always looking for new adventures and new worlds to conquer, snapped me up, ordered me to accompany her to the beach club, to the tennis court, to the riding stables. She gave me her clothes, her enthusiasms, her aching affection. The only miracle in this was that, despite the suddenness of her attentions, and the remarkable generosity of her family when importuned with my needs and requirements as Dorinda saw them, despite even the arrival of the glamorously derived Nellie, Dorinda's loyalty to me never faltered.

In time I came to see that my mother, schooled in a harsh world, was frustrated by this constancy. It belied the lessons she had determined to teach me, of the perfidy of friends, the danger of circumstances, the likelihood of disaster. And this lesson was reinforced and repeated, not only by my mother but by her four sisters, whose whole "take" on life was the prevention of disaster. Life was not to be lived, let alone experienced; it was to be outwitted.

Only three of the aunts actually imposed their views upon

me; the other one had run off with someone else's husband, and dared not show her face. Propriety was all. When, in college, I read George Eliot's *The Mill on the Floss*, I saw in Maggie Tulliver's aunts my own relations. But my mother, unlike Maggie's, was not weak. She was the oldest and the strongest of them all. The sisters were part of what could, no doubt, be called a matriarchy; certainly they had been produced by their mother, a woman of extraordinary power and attraction. Their father, apart from his inevitable part in the fertilization of eggs—and certainly I would have suggested even in my youth that these women were the result of parthenogenesis had I known the word—played no part in the family drama. My grandmother had early discovered that he was competent at nothing but drinking and throwing money away and she left him to it, supporting the family and directing its passage through life.

The three ever-present sisters—and I thought of them more as my mother's sisters than as my aunts, almost as though they were aspects of her, or a kind of chorus chanting again her pronouncements—were married, all of them to men who made good livings and were able to provide their wives with smart clothes, a good decorator, and vacations the need of which always mystified me, for they did nothing all year, having a maid and, when in due time they each produced two children, a "girl" who looked after them. That my mother was a kind of servant was a fact they were forced to overlook because she was so much the dominant figure in their lives that they could not operate without her. They lied about her work to their friends, recognizing perhaps that while they had "girls" to help out, in the world where my mother worked children had nannies (as Peggy Guggenheim wrote, often one for each child) and, later,

33

governesses. Dorinda was at the governess stage when we met, and from that governess I, together with Dorinda, learned to speak and read French. Fortunately, I was less quick at this, as at everything, than Dorinda; perhaps that was why I was never a threat in that way.

In the years between the time when Dorinda and I met and the time when Nellie came, books were the chief source of our fantasies and the major topic of conversation. I remember with particular clarity when we read Elizabeth Bowen's *The Death of the Heart*, and both dreamed that a filmmaker would decide to make a movie of that novel and cast one of us as Portia, the adolescent heroine. Neither of us had any doubt that, should we be spotted by a movie director as stars so often had been, or so magazines such as *Life* told us at the time, Dorinda would be the one. She was slim and ethereal-looking with good bone structure of the Garbo sort and wide-set blue eyes. I was fuller of figure, although athletic, and anything but ethereal. But we were, in school and after, together so constantly, I was able to imagine that some of Dorinda's qualities rubbed off on me.

Have I mentioned that Dorinda's family, at her earnest request, had arranged for her school to grant me a scholarship? Perhaps they took me because I might add an interesting, lower-class note, perhaps because Dorinda's family, having been generous in their donations, must be listened to, perhaps because the Head of the school, interviewing me, thought she spotted promise: I shall never know. But I transferred just before high school to Dorinda's school, known as Miss Hadley's, where we wore uniforms and did not, happily for me, compete about clothes. My mother used to say that the only competition seemed to be about who could be the sloppiest. I adored the school.

Of course we did not read anyone as contemporary as Elizabeth Bowen in class, but the library was encouraging about current fiction, so we were wonderfully up to date and yet, it occurs to me, read ''good'' books, well written, delicate, and sophisticated. If we missed much, we learned the sound, the precision, of proper English prose. How old-fashioned I, who have always been so radical, must sound.

I particularly recall Elizabeth Bowen because she had (I must have read this later) a profound sense of place. She said somewhere that place was more important to her than character; having become a storyteller myself, I recognize that place has never especially inspired me or moved me except as it can be evoked by a sudden, sharp memory. Descriptions of places always seemed to me tedious, and to this day I become impatient with authors who insist upon describing all the furnishings in a room before they will allow their characters to enter it or, once there, to speak. Yet I should describe the house on the New Jersey coast because it was, as a place, so central to our youth, and the years of our triumvirate.

The house and grounds occupied an entire block, the house at one end, the garage at the other, and enormous gardens and lawn between. In those days, the rich did not have swimming pools and tennis courts on their own property: they belonged to clubs for those purposes. Their homes were for relaxation. So, if there was to be a picnic under some trees on the lawn, a table would be set up, food brought out by the servants, and a cloth spread. The house itself was built for the summer: it had a porch on two sides, with rockers and swings. One entered the house always through the front door off the porch, into an enormous living room (as I thought of it), with a stair on one side sweeping upward to the bedroom floors; at the extreme top of the stairs was a skylight with stained glass; the living room was open to that skylight, which formed part of its ceiling. In the center of this room, in a comfortable chair, would sit Dorinda's grandfather, the maker of the fortune. As any of Dorinda's friends entered, he would greet them: "Hello, my dear!" and beckon them to him. Each of Dorinda's friends answered that beckoning only once for he would grab his victim, sit her on his lap, and begin to stroke her, gradually moving his hand toward her private parts, and where her breasts were beginning. After the first time, each of us learned to greet him cordially, while circling at a safe distance around his chair toward the staircase, or the dining room off to the back, well out of his reach.

I have often reflected since that Dorinda never warned her friends about her grandfather, but confirmed their experience with a sort of "now you know" shrug. What her motives were in the matter, whether she thought we all ought to find out for ourselves as the quickest way to useful knowledge, or whether she disliked mentioning the antics of the dirty old man, I never asked and never learned. I can only say that the one experience with him was not bad enough to be called child abuse—we were, after all, in the open in the middle of a busy house—and it taught me something about sex that seemed, thereafter, essential: men took it from you if they could. I found this not frightening, but useful knowledge, of the sort I doggedly collected.

Dorinda had a suite of rooms to herself; her French governess had one room, often empty in the summer as she took her vacation to France and then, as the war came, elsewhere; there was a room for a guest. Dorinda's own room, both here and in New York, was, at her request, fixed up as a sitting room. After Nellie came, she and I shared the twin beds in the guest room. In New York, Nellie had her own room, and I stayed overnight only occasionally. But my memories are, mainly, of the house on the Jersey shore.

In the evenings there, we neatened ourselves up for dinner, which was served in the large dining room with Grandpa at the head of the table. He used to interrupt the conversation with bursts of song and totally inappropriate observations, either to the conversation or the occasion, and at the end of every meal he would always struggle to his feet and make the same loud and tiresome remark about *that* meal being over. I always averted my eyes from this embarrassing, because unchanging, scene. But no one ever complained of his habits, or made him feel anything but the head of the household which, financially, he doubtless was. Dorinda's father now headed the business his father had made so successful—it had been founded in the previous generation as a small enterprise—and it is somehow characteristic of the time that I never knew what the business was. I remember thinking that they made money, which was true, God knows. Recently I asked Dorinda what the business had been—the family was long out of it—and she said that they had been investment bankers of some sort, so I had been largely right after all.

As soon as we heard of Nellie's arrival, we began to read the famous book by Emmanuel Foxx. He had written others, of course, before and after, but this was the one that had made him famous, the one they had to fight to get published in the United States and England. Dorinda and I had been too young at the time of the trial allowing the book's publication to take notice. Dorinda heard all about it at home;

37

her father was closely involved with the whole matter, and he was not a man to consider confidentiality a rational mode nor to temper his stories to the young. When Nellie was coming, therefore, Dorinda suddenly remembered the stories, and found a copy of the famous novel in the summer house: actually, the family had copies of all the first editions from many countries, and much of the conferencing at the time of the trial had taken place on the Jersey shore.

Because we were bookish, we had less trouble finding the salacious parts of the book than we might have had in 1941 at age fifteen. For the most part, the accounts of his heroine's thoughts were, to us, endlessly boring as, I suspect, they were to many. But he provided the reader with moments of heightened prose describing sexual experiences; we read these with enormous delight. Alone, I might have pretended to be unimpressed, even not to understand, but Dorinda's forthrightness made that impossible. So we smacked our lips, and thought of the delights that awaited us. They were nothing like the thoughts with which we had previously identified, of Elizabeth Bowen's Portia.

In those days, days hard to recall after the sexual and other revolutions of our time, it was repeatedly and annoyingly said of girls that they were "sweet sixteen and never been kissed." Dorinda and I snorted at this, although it partly described us: if not sweet, we had not "necked," as we all called it. Life offered far too few opportunities. But by the time we were sixteen, we were the triumvirate; we had all been kissed, and the next summer at the Jersey shore, we went to the dances arranged by the USO to meet sailors. No sexual adventures came of these dances, but we liked to ask the boys to the house for dinner three at a time, an intrusion that Dorinda's mother, as usual, took in her stride; there was always enough food. When we all were at dinner, Dorinda's grandfather would catch sight of their white uniforms somewhere around the second course, and start singing a naval song from Gilbert and Sullivan. We girls giggled and smirked at the sailor boys' discomfort. We felt like women of the world.

In the winters in New York my mother did not live "in," but shared an apartment with me in the lower floor of a private house between Columbus and Amsterdam avenues in the Eighties. It was a largely Irish neighborhood then, and Irish girls would shout at me from the stoops because, as was instantly evident to them, I was different. The degree to which I accepted this as a fact of life, to be borne but not reacted to either externally or internally, came to astonish me in later years. Perhaps the sneers of the Irish children did not impress me because it did not touch my real life, lived with Dorinda and Nellie.

That winter, the winter before Pearl Harbor, we began to have parties with boys in Dorinda's living room. Her parents willingly cleared out; her grandfather, who during the winters lived with his nurse in a hotel, had not to be considered. Not that we ever did consider him; he was like a domestic totem, bowed to, steered clear of, little noticed in the present demanding world of each day.

Where did the boys come from? I can scarcely remember. In Dorinda's circle, they were a source simply tapped, from boys' schools, her parents' friends' children, dancing classes; one of the boys—Len, the one with whom I early became paired off—had been picked up at a summer farm Dorinda had once visited, where he was working to save money for college. Did he and I immediately recognize each other as from a different class? He was to become my first, my sweetest, my only lover. When I was not yet sixteen, he and I half sat or lay on the couch or floor like the others, necking, kissing, to (can it have been always?) César Franck's only symphony.

The music was played on a Capehart, an unbelievably elegant record player. Those of us who did not have to put one record at a time on our players (and the records then were 78 rpm; it took four or five recorded on both sides for a symphony) had at best a device that dropped them in turn one upon the other; these records had, of course, been manufactured so that all of them were stacked to play on one side, then the lot turned over to play on the other. But as the records piled up they slipped and scratched, causing most of us to abandon these recordings in favor of the old-style records which we turned over and changed by hand.

But the Capehart, which occupied a huge cabinet, had its own special mechanism. Mechanical hands emerged and turned the record. After the record had been played on both sides, the hands flung it to the other end of the cabinet where it landed on a felt-covered slide. Sometimes the Capehart became angry—at the music, at us, at being overworked?—and it would fling the records across the room. We laughed and applauded and stacked them up again. I always mean to ask Dorinda or her mother what finally became of the Capehart. When long-playing records came in, it doubtless went the way of all obsolescent objects in our culture.

Nellie was very popular at our school and with our group; and life between the three of us, Dorinda, Nellie, and I, seemed an unending conversation of discovery about life and plans for our, as we then believed, unconventional futures. What did we imagine our lives would be? I have tried to remember what we said to each other, tried to hear our voices separately rather than melded, as they are when I recall them, into a chorus. Well, perhaps I should say chorus with leader, for Dorinda's was the dominating voice, the one who set our tone and orchestrated our debates. This was not only because her family and her money were supporting both Nellie and me; it was because we two were on the quiet side, and Dorinda was forthright: she knew what she wanted and what she meant to say. Neither Nellie nor I could ever have imagined, let alone prophesied, that Dorinda would revert to a conventional destiny. Not even Nellie's experience of Europe seemed more authentic than Dorinda's, since Dorinda had visited Europe, and had Europe visit her, all her life. And the only experience I could offer, of poverty and thrift, was not one I had any desire to emphasize.

What did we talk of all those hours? The imagined sex lives of our teachers, the actual lives of our classmates' families, at least as we had observed and interpreted them.

"Her father's had a mistress for years," Dorinda would say; I remember that discussion of a particularly rich and elegant family whose sad last offspring was in our class.

"What is a mistress?" Nellie asked. I remember that I too did not know what the term meant (however unbelievable that seems these days), and was glad that Nellie had asked.

"It's a concubine," Dorinda said, giving an explanation wholly satisfactory to our bookish selves.

"What do women have?" I remember asking. I hated the way men were the heroes of everything.

"Women take lovers," Dorinda said. "I know Nellie's mother did, before Nellie was born, of course." This last was added, quite illogically, to keep from hurting Nellie.

We never attacked each other, and argued only about principles.

"Even after," Nellie said, as though this was little more than a matter of correct information. "Everyone knew."

By that time, of course, we had all boned up on the works of Emmanuel Foxx, and we honored Nellie's paternal heritage. Only Len and I admitted to each other that we did not find Foxx's writing riveting. I was guilty about this: after all, he was writing about a woman, and, interested in women, I could find few enough books that portrayed them in other than romantic modes. Perhaps I sensed, without being wise enough to know, that what Foxx had produced was not a woman's thoughts, but a man's fantasy of a woman's thoughts. Despite Len and my doubts, which we kept to ourselves (my only disloyalty to Dorinda), Nellie existed in a golden glow whose reflection illuminated Dorinda almost as brightly, and even shone sufficiently on me to make me envied. I was consciously happy as part of the trio, and considered myself blessed. That is an emotion I read little of in other people's accounts of their youth, but for me it was quite simply a magic time.

By now, I was telling my mother almost nothing of my daily (or nightly) life, though no doubt she knew enough of that crowd to have her suspicions. She spoke to me openly and sternly about the dangers of pregnancy and of letting boys get the better of me. I did not want her advice nor, after parrying Dorinda's grandfather, did I need it. I intended to live my own life, take my experience where I might, and have a proud profession. Fortunately, Len was an honorable soul and did not challenge these naïve decisions; also Dorinda's sexual adventures provided enough vicarious experience to keep Nellie and me on the straight and narrow while we watched with delight and wonder Dorinda on her primrose path. So, at least in the beginning, I followed my mother's advice after all but, I assured myself, only coincidentally, and for my own reasons.

Sometime in 1955, as I was rushing around a department store (of which there were many in those days cheek by jowl along Fifth Avenue), I met Eleanor Goddard in the nightwear department. The publishing house for which I worked had decided to send me to London, and I recognized the need for decent pajamas of the sort all women then wore. (Oddly enough, nightgowns, or nothing, seemed to come back with the women's movement.) I was not preparing for a romantic encounter, but for the possible invitation to stay with someone, or to share a hotel room. It had been two years since I had seen Dorinda's mother, and I babbled most of this out when we had scarcely got past our surprised hellos. Dorinda's mother, listening in her quiet way to my rather long-winded account, latched on to only one word: London.

"I wonder if I might ask you to do me a kindness while you're there," she said.

"Of course," I said. "Anything." I did not think of Dorinda and her family as often as I used to, but I never lost the sense of owing them almost everything except my literal birth and first twelve years. I used sometimes to imagine how I could ever pay them back. Much older now, I understand that their gifts, freely given without sacrifice, were generous enough, but not nearly as lovely nor as dearly bought as the bare minimum, as I saw it, my mother provided for me.

"Gabrielle Foxx is still in London," Dorinda's mother

said. "Emmanuel's widow," she added after a moment, not wanting to assume I ought to know. She need not have worried; the story of Emmanuel Foxx and the beautiful aristocratic girl he had run off with were as unforgettable to me as any history I knew. "We haven't heard from her in a very long time. Emile used sometimes to write; Gabrielle was never a great writer. Might you drop in on her while you are in London?" Emile, I recalled after only a moment's effort—for he was fated from birth to be a minor player in the Foxx drama—was Emmanuel and Gabrielle's son and Nellie's father.

"Of course," I said again. She wrote the address out for me on a pad she carried in her purse (she was always organized, always prepared; how else could that complicated household be run; I had always understood that).

"I'll call you when I get back," I told her. "If there seems to be any sort of problem, I'll cable from London." But I knew, short of imminent death, I would save my story for when I returned. Talking face to face to Dorinda's mother and father about something so important as the Foxx family was not to be denied me. I saw little of Dorinda these days, but her family still held a kind of fascination for me that time could not lessen. "How is Dorinda?" I asked with a certain note of apology in my voice. I ought not to have had to ask.

"Fine. Quite wrapped up in being a mother."

Dorinda had transmogrified herself, as completely, I chose to think, as a prince under a spell becomes a frog. It was unlikely now that this frog would ever be recalled to earlier radiance with a kiss, or by any other means. From the wildest of rich, mad, daring young women, hungry for sex and reckless adventure, Dorinda had, all in one day, it seemed, ordained the end of her giddy youth. She had married a surgeon, a man so dull and pompous that one could scarcely bear to spend an evening with him except for Dorinda's sake, and produced two children within her first five years of marriage. The giddy joy she and Nellie and I had felt at being only children, bound to no siblings but each other, freely chosen, had somehow led Dorinda to deny her own offspring the same opportunity. Perhaps she feared where it might lead.

"Dorinda is pregnant again," her mother said. "I'm sure she'd be glad to hear from you." And thanking me again for my promise about Gabrielle Foxx, she left me to the contemplation of pajamas and a suitably ladylike robe. As I indicated my choice to the saleslady, I remembered Dorinda, like Virginia Woolf's Sally Seton, running naked through the halls of the Jersey house, daring her parents' proper guests to catch a glimpse. And now she had ended like Sally Seton, dully married, a lady, a mother several times over, all but unrecognizable.

Although we all three went to different colleges, we kept in close touch during those years; Nellie and I, for our different reasons, were hard-working, sober young women, content to have one boyfriend at a time ourselves yet eager to be stirred, amazed, sometimes horrified by Dorinda's accounts of her adventures. She had begun by sleeping with the chauffeur one summer at the Jersey shore. Her parents had bought her a small runabout—to this day I can render every inch of that car, although I have forgotten so many of the faces from that time. It was gray, a Ford coupe, as they were called, with room only for two (three at a squeeze) in the front, and a rumble seat in the back. Nothing, not convertibles nor the various status cars that have come and gone in the course of my life, ever carried one hundredth of the glamour of that small Ford coupe.

The car appeared on Dorinda's seventeenth birthday (always in the summer, always marked by glorious presents and celebrations; to this day, July 13th seems to me full of promise and nameless glee when I can scarcely remember the birthdays of those much closer to me now). The chauffeur was instructed to teach Dorinda to drive; he was a handsome young man, courteous and well mannered, doubtless holding that job because of some health reason, to earn money for his aging mother, something noble. I can't remember why he wasn't in the army; perhaps he had some unnoticeable but fatal illness—certainly it vastly increased his charms for us to think so.

Dorinda, eager to be rid of her virginity, seduced him in the car. When she told us about it, Nellie and I feared the nice young man would lose his job (that this was our fear tells me now a good deal about attitudes of the time), but we need not have worried. Dorinda got him to teach Nellie and me to drive. He behaved with perfect propriety toward the two of us, though we simultaneously dreaded (and hoped?) that he would exact the same price from us.

Dorinda's sexual adventures continued from the year of the Ford coupe, becoming ever more daring, ever more random and, it seemed to Nellie and me, undiscriminating. There was also at this time the occasional rich scion who dallied with Dorinda until she told him, as she always did sooner or later, that she was Jewish. (She did not look Jewish, and having a gentile mother was, in fact, not Jewish by Jewish law, but she could never resist shocking anyone. She did not marry a Jew, however, and passed serenely into the higher reaches of New York's WASP world, as it came to be called.)

It was at about this time when, as I now realize, Dorinda's mother must have begun to guess at her daughter's sexual exploits that she and I became closer. We were both, I now see, outsiders in that family into which Nellie was, after all, born; we were gentiles, we were conservative by nature, and made uncomfortable by flamboyant behavior. During our college years, I went to see Dorinda's mother, who had by this time asked me to call her Eleanor, whenever I came to New York. I used to contemplate the possibility that she was my mother, that I had been handed over to my housekeeping parent for mysterious reasons never to be known. Certainly we understood each other far better than either of us understood our assigned partners in the mother-daughter dyad.

I know now that Eleanor was basically a conservative, unquestioning person, readily accepting the mores of her own class and the class into which she had married. Even so, I gave her little enough credit for understanding much more than her duties as a wealthy man's wife. I know now that she, unlike my mother and Dorinda, comprehended the abyss I straddled because she straddled it herself. Then, I wanted more of life than Eleanor's rich woman's destiny— even though these women were supposed to be the freest, most handsomely endowed of all the women I saw in my youth. No matter what my feelings about my mother, I saw that she was, as a widow and working person, her own woman, even if employed by others. Eleanor worked just as hard at her glamorous life. Certainly she worried more, moment by moment, than my mother and seemed always invisibly to tremble with anxiety and fear. So I suppose I had some justification for thinking her incapable of autonomy or self-reliance. What was the point, I thought, of being rich if it only led to stress and anxiety? Eleanor worried before meals and after them, she worried about the yearly moves to and from the Jersey shore, she worried about the state of the country house, Sig's impulsively invited guests (no wonder there was always enough food for the sailors), and above all, I suspected, she worried about the richly born people with whom she had to interact as if her past had been like theirs.

Because I understood instinctively the terrors of Eleanor's life, it is easy enough to say now that I lacked a role model. Of course I did, but at least I had a chance at education, a chance to prepare myself, should I wish, for a nondomestic profession. That my mother ran houses for other women only made her a fool in my eyes; she was no less a domestic slave than the women she worked for. And, unlike Dorinda, I could not admire Hilda, who had married a famous man's son. She had still, I thought, followed one of those few narrow paths allowed to women, using her sex to buy her way into an interesting life. Looking back now, I am almost certain that my mother disapproved as heartily of Hilda's marriage to Emile as did Eleanor herself. But my mother never spoke to me about her views of the families she worked for, least of all the Goddards. And it was part of Eleanor's code never to convey this to anyone except, I now see, eventually and only by implication, to me.

Eleanor and her sister-in-law Hilda, who married Emile Foxx, came from wildly disparate backgrounds and classes, but they were alike in being denied a chance even to go to college, much less to prepare for a career not emphatically female. So Eleanor had the choice of training to be a nurse, a schoolteacher, or a secretary, and chose the latter because she had had enough of nursing and children as the oldest in her large family. And Hilda, rich, spoiled, indulged as the recipient of all the luxuries the well-off could afford, had only her beauty and sense of adventure, inevitably sexual, to suggest a way of life. When Eleanor and Hilda met as sisters-in-law, they shared nothing but the husband-brother (his devotion to his sister probably surpassed that to his wife) and the table around which they occasionally, at the Jersey house and for family celebrations, together sat.

At the time Eleanor and I spoke in the nightwear department Hilda had died two years ago from cancer. Hilda's was a life of almost catastrophic waste and misfortune, all arising from the necessity of the rich to raise their women to be beautiful objects of devotion without purpose and without sufficient discipline to live a life beyond the materialistic aims of their families.

These girls were educated at elegant schools, which never for a moment suggested to them the possibility of their undertaking a profession. Women worked only because they had to, and it was the pride of these successful men, as it was the pride of my mother's sisters' husbands, that their women need never lift a finger outside of their homes or the time they gave as charity in a noblesse oblige mood. My mother worked because my father, having died, could not support her. Had he deserted us, it would have come to the same thing. My aunts, like the daughters in the wealthy Jewish families for which my mother worked, had not gone to college. Either college was considered too expensive and unnecessary for women like my aunts and Eleanor, or too dangerous for women like Hilda. By the time of Dorinda and my generation, women of the upper middle class were, as an assumed right, sent to college by their wealthy fathers. I was able therefore to look back at that deprived generation of Hilda's and understand what her situation must have been, wherein her desperation lay. Her sexual escapades, unlike Dorinda's, lasted for life, as did her instability; it was almost as though if she stopped to ask herself what she was doing, she would vanish into thin air. And when the coming war found her in Europe, forced finally to think, to question her circumstances, she went mad. Dorinda's father had to have her anesthetized and brought to America under the care of two nurses aboard one of the last civilian ships to make the ocean crossing.

To Eleanor, Hilda must have seemed like a mutant, or a creature from an unknown species. There is a picture of them together in the garden of the New Jersey house, before Hilda had met Emile, when Eleanor had just become a Goddard daughter-in-law. They are standing with the grandfather, his arm around his beloved and beautiful daughter Hilda. Eleanor stands at their side, her hair carefully done, her clothes exactly right, her stance awkward. It would be two years before Dorinda and Nellie were conceived, Dorinda after much effort, Nellie almost as an incidental event. I too was yet to be born. It was impossible for me to look at that snapshot without placing the three of us, Dorinda, Nellie, and I, into a sort of cloud of the unborn hovering above the picture. What my mother's life was like at that time never interested me in the slightest.

The story of Dorinda's birth is easily enough told. She was conceived after many months of despair and born after an atrocious labor. Her father, Sig, finally shown the large, bruised female infant, snorted and said that she looked like a Jewish comedian. I knew this, because he had often told Dorinda who had told me. Yet I imagine him, with his careless ways, worrying at that very moment about his cherished sister Hilda, pregnant in France.

Eleanor had been Sig's secretary; perhaps he married her because she was docile, efficient, and orderly; perhaps because she would not sleep with him otherwise. Sig was so attractive that a woman refusing him was no doubt a novelty. Eleanor told me, in later years, that although the Goddards insisted as a matter of course that she hire a nursemaid for Dorinda, she used to follow the nurse along the streets at a discreet distance to make sure her child was safe. Occasionally, she would insist on taking Dorinda, in her elegant pram, out on her own. It was as though, she later told me, Dorinda knew she had someone controllable in charge. She would hold her breath in anger at whatever direction Eleanor was taking, and turn bluer and bluer before the eyes of her horrified mother, until Eleanor gave in and went where Dorinda wanted to go. Eleanor assumed, I don't know on what evidence, that the nurses never had this problem.

When the nurse had become a governess, certainly later still when I first knew Dorinda, Eleanor had learned to wear her robes of ladyhood more naturally. She was, in fact, a natural lady, but it took her some years to trust herself and her authority, at least with her servants and in the Goddard circle. I don't think she ever believed herself to have any control over Dorinda. She would tell me stories of Dorinda's triumph, rather as though this proved not so much her own falterings as Dorinda's spirit. She must have been the most astonished of us all when Dorinda suddenly turned conventional. It was almost as though her mother's genes suddenly sprang into action twenty years later.

In Europe, meanwhile, Hilda wore her beautiful clothes while moving with infinite grace and wealth in artistic circles. There were nightclubs, of course, and the gay life between the wars. Somehow, although I can picture everything else about the Goddards' life before I came into it, my imagination refuses to cross the ocean. I know only what Eleanor, Dorinda, Nellie, and the later biographies of Emmanuel Foxx told me—that Hilda, early into her European career, met Emmanuel Foxx and became, as had so many women, his slave. Hilda, who could not pick up her own underwear or scrawl letters on her own behalf, typed manuscripts for Foxx and helped him out in numerous ways, some costing only money, but others effort, tedium, and even pain.

Gabrielle, Emmanuel's wife, loathed Hilda from the first; more accurately, I suppose, she feared her: her beauty, her money, her fascination for Emmanuel. But in the end Emmanuel proved resistant to Hilda's charms, if not to her money or efforts. So she turned her brilliance upon Emmanuel and Gabrielle's twenty-year-old son, Emile. She was older than he, and far more practiced at the flirtation game. He had been dragged around Europe after his father, who was always in search of better conditions, better ways to pay the rent, more attentive women and patrons. Dorinda told me before Nellie came that Nellie, like her father, spoke four languages, all of them with a special precision that reveals the language as not one's own. Emile and Nellie were excellent linguists with no mother tongue. Nellie came to America and the Goddards so eagerly, not only because of the war, but because here was a place to which she might, at least for a few years, belong.

Shortly after Hilda and Emile started their affair, people

began referring to him as a gigolo. I suppose it was hard not to. In all the surviving photographs he stands with Hilda in a group, she at the center, he on the edge looking sulky and rather out of place. But she must have fascinated him with her beauty, her practiced arts of wiliness, her wealth, and her carelessness about the cost of anything. When she became pregnant, Emmanuel Foxx insisted that they marry; he wanted an heir, someone to carry on his name. Everyone assumed, including Emmanuel himself, that he wanted a male heir, but when Nellie was born he announced that, since the protagonist of his famous novel was a woman, it was only right that his heir be a woman also. She was named after the character in his great novel, but was always called Nellie by everyone who knew her.

Once Hilda had tired of posing for beautiful pictures with the newborn baby, she turned Nellie over to nurses. But Gabrielle, Emmanuel's wife, intervened. She took over her grandchild, an act of which Emmanuel heartily approved, and so Nellie lived with them for the most part, as did her father in the late thirties once he had tired of Hilda and his role as husband to a still wildly flirtatious woman. (Peggy Guggenheim was reputed to have insisted that her lovers try all the positions pictured on the walls of some building in Pompeii where women were not allowed to enter but into which Peggy Guggenheim had bribed her way. Whether this is true or not, it was Hilda's boast also. Doubtless new lovers were as essential to this frantic game as were new positions.) But although Nellie lived with her grandparents and her father, it was to her mother's family she gladly, eagerly came when she got the chance. Emmanuel wanted her safe; Emile had taken to drinking so constantly that his opinion was neither sought nor given. What Gabrielle

53

thought no one asked or perhaps cared. Nellie at least knew
that her grandmother would miss her, and used to write her
letters in which she tried to sound loving, but could scarcely
conceal how good a time she was having, how happy she
was to be in America with the Goddards, Dorinda, and me.

When I arrived in London later that year after meeting
Eleanor in the store, I wondered if Gabrielle would remember me as the third girl in Nellie's letters. I had thought of
Gabrielle so often over the years, had heard so much of her
from Nellie and from the Goddards, that I felt we could
meet as old acquaintances. If, of course, she was not too old
to find a place for me among her sad memories.

Upon Emmanuel Foxx's death, not long after Nellie's
departure for the States, Gabrielle dropped into obscurity.
Literary admirers and adorers put up with wives if they must
as part of the price of the noble man's presence. But without
the great author, a wife, unless she is literary executor and
a tight guarder of the reputation and literary leavings, like
the widow of T. S. Eliot, is as unregarded as his merest
belongings, more likely, indeed, considered fit only as rum-
mage.

As always, it was the Goddards who came to the rescue.
They sent Gabrielle a monthly check which they hoped but
hardly dared expect would not be spent largely on Emile's
alcoholic needs. And then, quite suddenly, Emile disappeared during the war, picked up, it was suspected, by the
Nazis who were by this time ruling Paris. There was some
hope that he had pulled himself together, stopped drinking,
joined the Resistance and either gone into hiding or been
killed heroically in some action against the Germans. But
no one could find out anything about him. Emile's disap-

pearance was, perhaps, the last straw for Gabrielle. She was alive; money reached her. This was all the Goddards were able to establish during the war.

After the liberation of France, Sig Goddard managed to learn that Gabrielle still lived in a part of the old Foxx apartment. She had been cared for by several gallant women who had considered Emmanuel Foxx the great writer of his time, but had few illusions about his character or his thought for the needs of his wife should she survive him. Genius makes its own rules, they admitted that, but others must look out for the nonliterary leavings of his genius. And, most moving of all, particularly, as Sig Goddard said in his usual sardonic manner, given the parsimony and penny-pinching of the French, a restaurant owner whose restaurant the Foxx family had often dined in before the war offered Gabrielle a free meal every day. Eleanor mentioned to me at our meeting that she had, characteristically, thanked the man and sent him a suitable gift.

There had been a real effort made to bring Gabrielle over for Dorinda's wedding. Nellie had telegraphed to London pleading with her to come. But she said she was too old, that Nellie must represent her. I think we all knew then that Nellie ought to go to London to see her grandmother.

It was a huge wedding, at the Harmonie Club, with Nellie and me as bridesmaids. My mother was also invited, and I was in a secret panic that she would do or say something to disgrace me, but in fact she behaved perfectly correctly, and even seemed to enjoy herself. My mother, whom I had never thought of as a dancer—the very last skill in the world one would expect of her—having been asked to waltz by some man as a kind gesture, proved herself so graceful and gay that she danced all during the wedding and allowed me, when in my embarrassment and trepidation I dared to look at her, to see what she might have been if some gaiety had been allowed or available in her life.

Her dancing that way shocked me for another, secret reason. I had always been, in private, a wild dancer, whirling around the room, my head full of fantasies, my body moving in a way no ballroom dancing could ever permit. Years later, when the young began dancing opposite one another, but each moving in his or her own way, I recognized the kind of social dancing that I might have been good at. But I could never follow a man in dancing; I always wanted to move faster, to go at my own pace. Oddly enough, as it seemed then but as I should have perceived as an omen, Dorinda had no trouble with ballroom dancing, moving in her partner's arms as though his leading her was all she wanted of life. I never mentioned my private wild dancing to my mother; I only danced when alone, with a record on and no one to see or hear me. Some time ago I stopped, and have never taken up dancing again. Perhaps walking, to which I am addicted, took its place, perhaps the fantasies that accompanied my dancing receded with the years. At Dorinda's wedding, I danced a few obligatory rounds, and then sat at the table drinking champagne and trying not to watch my mother, unable not to watch her.

The Harmonie Club, where the wedding was held, was and probably still is—I have never taken the time to notice—at 60th Street off Fifth Avenue. It was a club for wealthy Jews who were not accepted at the usual clubs suitable to their social class. The club, I remember Dorinda telling me, took only German Jews, never Eastern European, and was very strict in its membership standards. Dorinda, dressed in a gorgeous bridal gown, walked down the aisle on her father's arm as though there had never been a gray Ford coupe or the men of her college years, with Nellie and me right behind her in matching pale-blue gowns paid for, needless to say, by the Goddards.

The groom waited in full regalia with his equally boring best man and claimed her the way they did in the movies of our childhood, but neither Nellie nor I was fooled. He hated us, and Dorinda's separation from us began with her wedding. But, as it happened, Nellie was off to London to visit her grandmother after Dorinda's wedding, a trip to London for which the Goddards paid, and I was to begin work as an assistant editor, really a secretary, in the publishing business, a job found for me, needless again to say, by the Goddards.

Dorinda walked down the aisle into the arms of her stuffy surgeon-to-be and out of the intimacy Nellie and I had offered her for the better part of our lives.

As I marched down the aisle behind Dorinda I revolved the ring on my right hand as a kind of talisman, signifying all that the Goddards and Dorinda had meant to me. It was—it still is—a Jensen ring, from the old days when the Jensen store was on Fifth Avenue and sold what I thought the most beautiful jewelry in the world. For my sixteenth birthday, the birthday after the night with the Capehart, the night I met Len, Dorinda and her mother went with me to buy me a ring. I chose the same ring Dorinda already had; the Jensen models were famous, and available year after year. The silver in the ring was carved with leaves, and the stone was a moonstone; I had always admired Dorinda's, had always longed for just that ring. I remember, though I politely pretended not to hear, that it cost thirty-five dollars, a huge sum then, almost unbelievable now. I left the store with the ring, vowing never to remove it; indeed, I have not removed it for long. It contained, so I fancied, all of our youth, for I had read some such phrase in a novel.

So I turned the ring on my finger walking down the aisle at Dorinda's wedding, perhaps to distract me from the farce in which I was taking part; I suddenly remembered also one of the first nights I spent with Dorinda in New York, after my first summer with her. The Goddards had taken us all in a taxi to Rumpelmayer's, and while we were ordering our sodas, a taxi driver came up, led by the manager, to say he had found my purse in his cab after he had left us off. I claimed, ashamed and guilty, the brown cloth bag he held out, first to Dorinda, then to me. I remember Mr. Goddard reaching into his pocket for some money with which to tip the driver. I knew my purse, which was an old one of my mother's, was worth less than the tip.

And there was another memory, too, which followed that one. It was of Dorinda's birthday party, that first summer. All the daughters of the families at the shore were invited. And each of us found, at our places when we finally sat down for dinner, a pencil box with our names in gold on the cover. When the box was opened, there was a row of pencils, each with a name. My box had my name. The pencils had my name. I kept the pencils and the box for years. It was Eleanor, of course, who had planned it all, who had included me.

It was Eleanor I would be repaying by doing my task in London well. Or, the realist in me added, by doing it at all.

My trip to London was hardly as glamorous as it sounded. I was being sent to assist a man who had been my boss in New York, but who had moved to London in the course of marital upheavals that were the riveting subject of gossip then, and about which I remember nothing. He had at first been considering moving to Paris to set up a French publishing office but, to my infinite relief, he had chosen London instead.

By the time I joined him there, my publishing career had already declared itself as in the business, not the literary or editorial, end. I was very good at figures, very efficient and quick, just like my mother, though such a thought would hardly have occurred to me. I housekept for publishers instead of for Our Crowd and the other rich. There was, I suppose I now see, very little difference.

Paris has never held any particular delights for me. I recognize the amazement such a statement evokes, but I am one of those who seems somehow never to have been part of the convictions of a generation or culture. I remember once reading about Irwin Edman, who had been young in the twenties, and he said his youth had been nothing like the flaming years he always read about. True, he was a philosopher, and perhaps had not found Scott Fitzgerald a spokesman for his desires or ambitions.

I have never been much of a traveler, and though I have loved cities, Paris is not a city, or so it seemed to me, for a lonely woman looking for streets in which to walk and bookstores (replete, of course, with books old and new in the English language) in which to browse. London is such a city; so was New York in those days. In Paris, one seemed always to be on the outside. Nor, I suspected, would that change if I went there on business; people might have to talk to me in a businesslike way, answer my questions, discuss relevant matters, but I doubted that such would prove to be the case. I spoke French, but with a heavy American accent.

The whole language of sexuality, so essential to French interchanges of all sorts, was unknown to me, nor did I honor it. I had found the French, during my one visit there a few years before, to be operating, in their attitudes toward money, sex, intellectual (as opposed to practical) ideas, clothes, and food, on a plane altogether too elevated for me. I see now that it was not my accent alone which ostracized me; it was also my total indifference to the many signs I missed, the many gestures I scorned. Blunt people have never recommended themselves to the French. When, later, I read the books of Nancy Mitford, I understood why I was destined always to be desolate in France. I enjoyed her writings, but knew that in her world, I would have been one of the clumsy ones caricatured in her novels.

I had even been in love the time I had spent in Paris, had met Len there again, had made that kind of young, frantic love, interrupted only by meals and idyllic walks under the chestnut trees. We loved, we walked entwined, but we did not admire the chestnut trees, pollarded and, in our view, tortured. The weather seemed to us gray, wet, and dark. We found the waiters supercilious and unkind. Frenchmen at nearby tables, overhearing us, insisted on telling us what was the matter with America. I was very glad my adulterous boss had decided on London, and doubly grateful when I was enabled, thereby, to do a favor for Eleanor and to enter, once more, into the affairs of her fascinating family, the family into which she had, perhaps so unhappily, married.

It was unclear that Gabrielle's marriage had been any easier than Eleanor's to bear. Yet she had run off with Emmanuel to Paris, dizzy with rapture, giddy with a kind of joy I had never known, nor, I secretly thought, wanted to.

It would be many years before I discovered that, as some Frenchman had said in an aphorism I found, among French aphorisms, uniquely accurate, there are those who love and those who consent to be loved. That rapture, that dizziness, belongs only to those who love, and the price they pay, the price Gabrielle had paid, seemed to me too high. It was later, when I came to this understanding, that I began to wonder if Eleanor had loved as Gabrielle had loved. Of course, I thought, that is the only explanation. And like Gabrielle, she had lived to experience the perils of marrying the object of one's passion.

Gabrielle's family cut her off without a shilling, as was thought only proper. She laughed in their faces. I suppose the life in Paris was attractive, with its artists, its expatriates, its life on the Left Bank. But it is one thing to be a careless Hemingway; it is quite another to try and manage a household and a child on the irregular earnings of a genius. Gabrielle was patronized, anxious, and in exile. But she seldom went back to London even when Emmanuel did, and though she was supposed to have made overtures to her family, these were never reciprocated.

The Goddards never knew quite why she had returned. She wrote them only that she was now living in rooms in Kensington, address provided so that the allowance could be sent, and hoped they were well; she was as ever grateful to them for their kindness. Eleanor had once told me there was nothing in Gabrielle's gratitude to suggest that the Goddards were providing more than her due. I was still too uncertain of my own gratitude to the Goddards to be able to judge Gabrielle's. I liked to think that my gratitude was uncomplicated, but my moments of resentment, however disguised as resentment at Dorinda for having turned out so disappointingly, warned me that a high moral tone toward Gabrielle was hardly justified.

The romantic story of Emmanuel and Gabrielle was as well known to me as any romance in literature—and literature comprises more of romance than of reality. If Romeo and Juliet had not died at the end of the play, how would they have lived? Did Shakespeare suggest, in *The Winter's Tale*, that a man can love his wife twenty years hence only if she is preserved in the fullness of her twenty-year-old beauty? Emmanuel and Gabrielle were almost Shakespearean in their love, or so it seemed still in 1955 when I went in search of sixty-six-year-old Gabrielle. Her son was dead; her husband was dead, after a short, painful, ultimately fatal illness; her granddaughter was an ocean away. Only I, the least connected to her of the three in our generation, was on my way to visit. Gloomy enough she might be, but still, even I expected her to be redolent of a great love. I had read somewhere that the old looked backward into the past, rediscovering and reliving. What a great past to have, what a great love. True, I would have wanted no such love for myself. But if one had to fling oneself thoughtlessly, carelessly, into the torrent of passion, how much better that passion's object should be a great writer, the great creator of a female hero.

Gabrielle had met Emmanuel when she was sixteen. It was always assumed, on the basis of family (Goddard) gossip, that she had allowed him "everything" on their first encounter. Emmanuel had been a visitor at Gabrielle's family home, a huge castlelike place (it may have become grander in the telling), brought there by one of Gabrielle's brothers who introduced Emmanuel as the great writer of the future. How often are such introductions prophetic? If

Emmanuel was not yet a great writer, he was already a man of extraordinary appeal, especially to women; a man, I have always supposed, like Rodin, or Augustus John, larger than life, large in his form and in his claims on life. Gabrielle adored him at first sight. "Whoever loved who loved not at first sight?" I have always assumed that Marlowe's line (my view is reinforced by the context in which Shakespeare quotes it) applies only to philanderers or those who know nothing of marriage.

She offered to show him the park, the lake with the ducks, the wild garden, and lay with him under a grove of beech trees, in the dappled shade beneath their thick leaves. When she ran off with him to Paris shortly thereafter, she must have been already pregnant with Emile, who was born nine months later. They were married in Paris by an official when they knew her to be carrying a child. Emmanuel had not been caught in marriage before, but this was (so the Goddards said) the first, or at any rate the youngest, virgin he had taken, and this fact convinced him that she was bearing his son and heir to carry on his name. Perhaps because Emile was such a disappointment, he welcomed Nellie's gender; that, at least, was my surmise.

Gabrielle's family was utterly unforgiving. Her father followed her to Paris, but when he caught up to the fleeing couple, which took some weeks, Emmanuel told him Gabrielle was pregnant and about to be married. The father, according to Goddard legend, announced that from that moment on he had no daughter, turned on his heel and departed. I always wondered if the brothers had made any attempt to see her—they were older, and certainly had some money of their own—but apparently they were conventional, or as jealous of family position as their parents.

Gabrielle's mother died soon after—from a broken heart, the Goddards assured me. She had loved her daughter, and blamed herself. Had she lived she might have understood Gabrielle's impulses, and supported her later in life. But she was wholly under her husband's thumb, and lost, with Gabrielle's elopement, her only reason for living. A romantic story, if ever there was one.

The Goddards supposed, on whatever evidence supported their wonderful stories of Emmanuel Foxx, that Gabrielle had, from time to time, written to her relatives for help, but none was forthcoming. Her letters, in the best English manner, were returned unopened. A second baby was stillborn, and the Foxxes had no more children. Considering the mess they made of Emile, that was probably just as well, or so I thought in 1955 in my arrogantly intolerant and jejune way.

But what, I remembered having asked Dorinda sometime after Nellie arrived, did they do in the war? I prided myself on being the historian in the group, tidy with facts as I liked to think myself, and aware that my father had been in the war before he ever met my mother. Dorinda did not know, but she asked at dinner, and her father said that Emmanuel had been almost forty at the time of the war, not conscripted by the French at first, and eventually found to have a heart murmur and an ulcer, which kept him out of the army. He retreated to the French countryside with his family, and continued to work on his novel, of far more importance, in his opinion, than the war.

One of Gabrielle's brothers was killed, and the other wounded, but that did not soften her father's heart, nor that of the surviving brother. Gabrielle helped Emmanuel with his writing, and tried to find enough food for him and the boy. It must have been a hard time. When I tried to picture it, I always thought of what I heard of the French country-side in World War II movies and stories, so that, in a strange way, Emile as a boy in one war and Emile as a member of the Resistance in another blurred in my mind.

The demands of my boss in London were many, and my time was filled with helping him to set up his office there and generally playing what was, in the fifties, considered the proper role of a woman assistant to an editor: the role of wife. Academic wives played the same role, of course, often to an extent unknown or unsuspected at the time. I well remember when, many years later, Queenie Leavis, the wife of that most terrifying and influential critic of his time, F. R. Leavis, admitted in an interview years after his death that she had done all the research for his famous books and written the greater part of them. So we who assisted the male publishers and writers did the research and typing and sometimes the writing, leaving them to get the credit and scurry about, meeting people. In those days *Time* and *Life* magazines were widely read, and on their staffs the men were the writers; the women, banned from that title, were "researchers." In my case, I eventually ran the office of the top men, not only as a secretary (they had a secretary separate from me) but as chief accountant, publicist, and, in many cases, decision maker.

It was thus not until I had been in London several weeks that I attempted to telephone Gabrielle, requesting an appointment. She turned out not to be, as the English said, "on" the telephone. Not to be on the telephone was less surprising then, less unusual than it would be now, but still amazing to my American self. I was forced, therefore, to write a letter, which, the blessed English mails not yet having achieved, like postal service everywhere else, their nadir, reached Gabrielle in the morning. She wrote an answer immediately which reached me the same afternoon, perhaps, as I look back on it now, the most unlikely event of all, looked at from this time to that. She asked me to come and see her at three o'clock the next day. Leaving my boss in a frenzy I could well imagine but did not go into the office to witness, I took the day off, walking the streets to think what I would say, to plan how I would begin my letter to Eleanor, and to buy some delicacies for Gabrielle.

I discovered her home was a ground-floor flat in a converted house on the edge of Kensington which the landlady, whom I met when I rang the bell, declared to be really in Knightsbridge. The landlady had lain in wait for me, Gabrielle's first visitor ever. Gabrielle must have told her I was coming, but little else. My American accent in no way precluded her immediate assumption that I was family; perhaps she thought I was Nellie. She told me how worried she was about Gabrielle, who never stirred from her rooms, who paid the "girl" to get her groceries and other necessities, who really was not the sort of lodger she, the landlady, really wanted, but after all the money came regular, didn't it, and you couldn't just put the poor thing out on the streets. Still chattering, she led me down the hall and past a stairway to Gabrielle's door. I thanked her, and stood there, staring her down, forcing her to leave me before I knocked. I wanted to be alone when I faced Gabrielle.

When I finally saw her, when Gabrielle opened the door and stood aside for me to enter, she claimed my attention with a sudden pungency no one, not even Nellie when she arrived in America, not even Dorinda when I first saw her, had equaled. All of that, I now understood, had been preparation for this moment. My life was, after all, more like a romance than a realistic biography. I had often thought about this, and discussed it inwardly, as I discussed most things once Dorinda resigned (as I saw it) from our childhood, once Dorinda and Nellie and I were separated. It is in romances, in fairy stories, in the kind of tales girls imagine, that events happen, fetching the young woman from her mundane destiny and placing her in a different, richer, more adventurous world. So it had happened to me: first, the Goddards, then Nellie, now Gabrielle. There was, furthermore, a reason why it was persistent, slightly dull, hardworking I, Anne, to whom all this happened, rather than Dorinda or Nellie, who seemed so much more obviously chosen by destiny for a starring role. Gabrielle required someone receptive like me. Eleanor, I surmised, would have done, but Eleanor was too entangled in her husband's life, too ancillary, too much a creature of the Goddards.

To me, just short of thirty, Gabrielle looked old and disreputable that day when I first caught sight of her. That is the right phrase: "caught sight of her." As though I had her at last in my vision, captured from my imagination. No doubt I had passed each day in New York or London women of sixty-six whom I would have thought neither old nor haggard because cosmetics and dieting had preserved their youthful appearance. Gabrielle looked every year and more of her age. It did not take me long, however, to discover her vitality, the vigor that is not the imitation of youth, the passing as young, but is genuine, having nothing to do with the impersonation of youth as fashionable women represented it. Gabrielle's hair, a mottled gray and white, had been cut off at her ears; I was conventional enough at that first meeting to yearn on her behalf for a "good" haircut.

She wore a long, formless dress, with an old cardigan over it: this house, like all English houses at that time, was cold. Her feet, with stockings of some thickish, peasanty material, were in what looked like men's slippers; her hands were large, with closely clipped nails and thickish fingers. All this I took in at a glance, without the words, as a revelation. Why is it that figures who appear in revelations are always beautiful, like angels? Why for that matter do we think of angels as always beautiful? I do not mean I instantly thought of Gabrielle as an angel; I mean that something in me assented to her, something recognized her, something said: "So here you are."

"Come in, then," she said. Her accent was pure upper-class English, the sort you hear less of now in England than you did then. In those days all the announcers on the BBC talked with Oxford accents; the Beatles, like the now ubiquitous intonations from Australia, Yorkshire, the Midlands, the East End, were in the future. Yet the purity of her speech struck me even at that time.

There was an electric fire in the fireplace, into which she popped a coin taken from a dish of them on a table nearby. I understood from that action that she kept her money for what mattered to her: warmth, a large room, her own bathroom, tips for the "girl" who fetched food and other items. She did not waste it on appearances or what did not directly serve. She had a radio, on which, in a few hours, she would listen to the news, and, in the evening, to music. Even at first glance, hers seemed to me a remarkably sensible arrangement.

My plan had been to ask her out to dinner; I relinquished it almost immediately. Her life was here and nowhere else. She had access to a garden in the back belonging to all the houses surrounding it. I supposed, or chose to believe, that she went out there from time to time to catch a breath of air. When I asked her, she told me that she stood at the open window sometimes at night, but never went out in the day. There were children there for whom she was a natural victim: she seemed to accept this as inevitable. She did not like children. As she said this, I realized that I did not like children either, had not even liked them when I was a child, except for Dorinda and Nellie, who were not children but, like me, small adults waiting for their transformation.

"Sit down," she said. I sat in a chair on the other side of the fireplace with its electric bars, a chair she had clearly put there for me before my arrival. There was no permanent need for two chairs by the heat. I sat down, still in my coat: the room was far from warm. "How is Nellie?" she asked.

"Nellie's fine," I said. "Just fine." It seemed inadequate as a response let alone as news, but she accepted it. Nellie, with her quiver of languages, had gone to work for an international bank and was doing very well. Like me, she had not married, seeing it as a trap. Neither she nor I had been fooled by the marriages of the world Dorinda belonged to; only Dorinda had been fooled by that. Perhaps one needed my mother and Hilda as models in order to have sufficient strength to avoid marriage, which every woman of our generation pursued as the golden fleece it so obviously, to them, was.

"Single like you," she said, echoing my thoughts. "Working; supporting herself. Good girl. And she made use of her languages, which Emile only saw as depriving him of a mother tongue. It broke my heart to let her go to America, but I knew if she stayed with me she would be doomed like me. Like Emile."

"Are you still doomed?" I asked. I have often, again and again, thought back to that question and why I asked it. It came to me as an inspiration. Inspiration is rare: a form of telepathy, or insight, a revelation that may be unique in a lifetime, requiring a lifetime's preparation. Certainly everything in my life had prepared me to ask, as though inspired, that question.

"No," she said. "I'm not. That's why I agreed to see you. You are the messenger."

Of course, being not yet thirty, I wondered for one frightful moment if she were mad. She must have seen that speculation in my face. "Perhaps more than a messenger," she said. "Perhaps a friend. You are exactly Nellie's age," she added in what was clearly, for her, a sequitur. "Would you like some tea?"

I accepted the tea gladly, real English tea, strong, with milk in it. She had, I now noticed, a kettle on a hot plate. We sipped our tea, and looked at one another; I had a sense of possibility that nothing, not even coming to live with Dorinda, had given me. I waited for her to speak, just to hear her voice, not expecting at this point anything profound.

"Foxx used to say the English upper classes drink tea as a sacrament. He was right; he was always right about the English classes. It's certainly better than wine; it's nobody's blood except the lower classes', no savior mixed up with it." And she let out a hoot. For the first time I saw her smile, reassuring me after the loud sound. Hers was a smile of overwhelming sweetness, redeeming the chopped-off hair and the ruined English skin filled with tiny broken veins; a smile of love and intelligence, rare as large rubies. I sipped my tea and a sensation of pure pleasure swept over me, like a rush of contentment, but far more pervasive than contentment, joy I suppose. When my mother went through the menopause she suffered from hot flashes; she described them as subsuming her, capturing her body as thoroughly as pleasure might, if only hot flashes were pleasure. Subsumed, I felt that pleasure now.

We did not hurry. I had placed my bag of delicacies on the floor soon after I entered, and I never knew what became of them. Perhaps Gabrielle gave them to the landlady, or to the "girl." I never saw Gabrielle eat, she did not invite me to a meal, I did not think of food when I was with her. We only drank tea, endless cups of it. Now I sat, drinking my tea and looking around the large room.

There were papers everywhere, on every chair, table, even next to the hot plate, in fact on every surface, including most of the floor. I had followed the path between the stacks of paper to the electric heater and the chairs almost by instinct; I was used to this sort of disorder; Dorinda had never put anything away, and I had to battle with myself at first to restrain the sense of tidiness imbibed with my mother's milk. Gabrielle took it for granted that, once having looked around, I would understand that this was not disorder but discovery, and the ordering of her life.

"They have started coming again," she said. "All those scholars, all those academic snoopers, hoping for letters, for memories, for my stories. You're the only one I've agreed to see. The landlady acts as though she does me a favor, letting me live here. Perhaps she could get more for this set of rooms. But I bribe her, all the time, with money and anything else (her eyes went to my bag from Fortnum

and Mason.) And she turns them all away; all but you. I told
her to let you in. The truth is, until you came, I couldn't
decide if it was you or Nellie. I'm glad it's you; Nellie has
her life to get on with."

I don't know why I failed to find offensive this assumption about my life as being something there was no need to
get on with. Partly because it was true: I pretended greater
interest in the world of publishing than I felt or, if not
greater interest, greater commitment. Also, I had always the
sense of awaiting a destiny, and this might be it.

"They are Foxx's letters?" I asked.

"Some. They are mostly my letters, letters I wrote him
every day for years, putting down my thoughts, my passions, my fantasies, sexual fantasies mostly. Telling him
how I thought of arousing him, recalling the excitement, the
frenzy of doing many things I never really did. He let me
write it instead of doing it; he said I was the most devoted
to the missionary position of anyone he had ever met. The
truth is, it was, finally, the easiest way."

"But you were so rarely apart." I had read what biographies there were; I was fully informed on all that was
known of Foxx, his life, and his passionate heroine. The
various outré sexual acts he had demanded of his heroine,
acts she had performed with passionate commitment and
enjoyment, floated into my mind. I tried to attach them, at
however distant a time, to this large woman sitting across
from me in her felt slippers and cardigan.

"We were never apart. He dragged me with him all over
Europe. He said I was his muse. Ha! I wrote each day in my
room; he locked me in. He wouldn't even let me go to the
baby if he cried. I learned to write very fast."

"And these are the letters?"

"Yes, mostly letters. I can scarcely bring myself to read them over. I have thought of burning them."

"Burning them! Oh, you mustn't; that would be a sacrilege."

"Why?" she demanded. "Tell me why!"

I must not remain silent, I knew. I must not hesitate. I must not say the wrong thing. "Because they *are* the words of a woman," I said. "They are your words. Why should the world think they are his?"

I had said the right thing. Later I would wonder if those words forced from her were indeed her words, or, like the words of masochistic women in pornographic novels, men's fantasies, really, women saying what men wanted them to say, pretending to feel what men wanted them to feel. But I did not mention this. It was always possible that there was more than sex acts here, that there were thoughts, ambitions, hidden hopes. After all, Foxx's heroine had wild ambitions, manly dreams, even the love of women.

For some reason I thought of Dorinda at that moment, of her wild girlhood, of her frenzied pursuit of experience, mostly sexual, of the conventions in which she had immured herself. Her wedding had indeed been a rite of passage, an initiation into proper womanhood. Why had I not thought of that then?

"Have more tea," Gabrielle said. She was, I knew, as she shuffled over to the kettle—her felt slippers were too large for her—deciding what next. Eventually, she decided on the next day. I must come tomorrow. At teatime. We would talk more then.

And so, without more tea, I was dismissed. Gabrielle turned from the kettle. But her face was kind; she smiled. I had no choice, although I did not want to go. I rose, still in my coat, gathered up my purse, and walked through the door she held open for me. I wanted to stay, but I could not find a reason to do so.

"I'll see you tomorrow," I said.

"Tomorrow," she answered, giving me a wave before she shut the door to her apartment.

The landlady was waiting for me. "Fine, is she?" she asked.

"Has she been ill?" I answered in what I hoped was a partly patrician manner.

"Oh, yes," the landlady said. "She has fits. Very queer, she becomes, very queer indeed. Well, you'll be here to see to her now. Her granddaughter, that's right, innit?"

I left because Gabrielle wanted me to, but with a terrible premonition that no call upon rationality that night or the following day could assuage.

I arrived the next day as early as could possibly be considered time for tea. The landlady was waiting for me.

"She was on the floor; the girl and I got her onto her bed, I'll never know how and that's the truth. She wouldn't let no one come, she won't drink nothing. She just wants to talk with you. She wanted the girl to go and fetch you, but I didn't know where you were staying, did I? We've been watching out for you, I can tell you."

She tried to come into Gabrielle's rooms with me, but I pushed her back, gently I hoped, and closed the door. Gabrielle was pale; she looked ill, her breathing was in short gasps, and there seemed to my horrified ears to be a sort of rumbling, a rasp, with each breath. She pulled at my sleeve, making me sit beside her on the bed.

"Take the papers. All of them. I've written it out for the

landlady, I wrote it before, I had only to put in your name last night. Don't leave without the papers. There are sacks, enough of them. Pack up the papers.'' She pointed to a sack near her chair; I could see that she had begun packing the papers into it, probably last night. She had overdone it and collapsed.

"You're only sixty-six years old," I said, as though I were pleading with her to reconsider her arithmetic and with it her illness. She ignored me.

"Pack them all up," she said. "Take them all away with you tonight. Tell them to get you a taxi. Pay them well, very well. The landlady, the girl, the taxi man. They will do what you want for money. Here."

She plucked at her skirt, indicating, as I soon understood, her pocket. I reached into it with her encouragement and removed a large packet of bank notes. This was, of course, before England went onto the metric system. I mention that here because the old English money had a kind of magic to it, it was like play money to me, it was the stuff of dreams, which the new pound notes, five- and ten-pound notes, never would be.

I nodded my agreement.

"Take them somewhere," she said. "Maybe another country. I don't have the money. Have you the money?" She was frantic now. I told her that I had the money; that I would take the papers to a bank somewhere safe, perhaps to a bank in Zurich, Switzerland—in my own frenzy, Switzerland and bank vaults collided in my mind and stuck there together. I told her that I would put them in a large safety-deposit box—a vault, as I seemed determined to call it. "Do it now! Pack them up! I want to watch you."

I did it. I have played that scene over and over in the

75

years that followed, watched myself gather up the papers and stuff them into the canvas sacks she had acquired. I seemed to myself even then to be playing a scene from a war movie, working with desperation, the Gestapo at my heels, threatening to descend at any moment. But there was no Gestapo. And the landlady would have done anything for the money I gave her. She could see I was not trying to carry off her furniture; what did she care about papers? She was delighted to be part of the drama. Later, I realized that she might have been one of those moral, law-abiding English women who insist on calling the police, on making sure everything is just so. Never before or since have I been so grateful for perfidy. How could she know I was not robbing Gabrielle, not stripping her of her most valued possessions? True, Gabrielle appeared to have condoned my actions, but by now she was breathing with even more difficulty, keeping her eyes closed most of the time, until, suddenly, she would seem to become panic-stricken and then, seeing me, would be reassured that I was there, that this was what she wanted.

When I had finished with the packing, I took Gabrielle's hand; I told her I would be back to see her tomorrow, perhaps later tonight.

"No," she said. "Go now, go as soon as ever you can. As soon as ever you can." And she closed her eyes.

We called a taxi and put Gabrielle's two canvas sacks into it; I rewarded the landlady with yet more money. Throughout the ride I sat in the taxi clinging to the sacks as though someone might hold up the taxi and claim them. After getting them up to the room in a bed-and-breakfast place in which I was staying, I relaxed a bit, reminding

76

myself that there was no Gestapo, that few people would be interested in the contents of Gabrielle's treasure.

I found a bank the next morning and rented a vault. I put the papers into it; the sacks would not fit. It seemed pointless to keep them, but I managed to fit them one inside the other and brought them back with me to my room. Later, I almost discarded them, realizing their inadequacy as totems. In the end I decided to keep them, because they were Gabrielle's. Feeling a bit silly, I kept them for that reason, and I have them still.

Once my mission was completed at the bank, I thought of writing Gabrielle, of sending a telegram saying MISSION ACCOMPLISHED, but she had warned me: "No messages; no messages." I was, as you must be reading this, certain that she would soon be dead, but she did not die then. The landlady, unable to rouse her, had called an ambulance and Gabrielle went to the hospital in an unconscious state from which she never really awakened. I had by this time cabled Eleanor, as I had promised, and the money came for a good nursing home.

I later visited Gabrielle there. They were kind enough to her, but she never knew where she was. I would sit, holding her hand, staying on in England days, then weeks, after my job required it, hoping she would speak. Sometimes, rarely, her hand moved, with the slightest pressure, in mine. But, finally, I came to terms with the fact that there was nothing further I could accomplish.

I never saw Gabrielle again. Eleanor came over to England to visit her just after I had gone back to the States. Later, Eleanor told me that the sisters at the nursing home had reported Gabrielle's asking for Nellie, sometimes, even when she seemed asleep, calling out for Nellie. But when Nellie went to the nursing home, Gabrielle did not recognize her.

Gabrielle died some years later. I have continued to pay the rent on the vault in the London bank. I was able to return to my old job in the publishing firm; I was too good to let go, and women could be paid so little then, and given so much responsibility and so little recognition, that the publishers would have been foolish not to take me back.

Part Three

Three

KATE had made her fatal leap into biography early
enough in the spring semester to request a leave without pay for the following year. The university had no hes-
itation in granting it. Financial stringencies made welcome
the saving of a full professor's salary, her work to be un-
dertaken by an adjunct at a fee that would, figured hourly,
have failed to achieve the minimum wage. Kate had done
her share of these stints in her life, and knew their advantages: the chance to work in a new place, meet new colleagues, new students; the chance to try out a new course or
test an old one against new questions; the chance to explore
a new neighborhood, a new campus.

Taking a leave without pay was rather like dying for a
time, never sure that the university would ever refind one's
records, or resist the temptation to give one's office to someone else. One knew it was not death only because one had

to prepay one's own medical insurance, and make complex arrangements about one's mail. She would begin working on the biography June first. Meanwhile, she would, when she found the time, nose around, as she put it to herself. The question was: where to begin nosing?

Russell Baker had, he reported, once announced to his wife: "I'm going upstairs to invent the story of my life." Kate echoed him to Reed: "I'm going to invent the story of Gabrielle's life. But, like a good biographer, I shall search for the evidence to substantiate my interpretations."

"Like a good detective, too," Reed had answered. "You never fail to astonish me; it's the reason I married you, in case you didn't know. You're the only person I know well who continues to surprise me. Most people confine themselves to adequately fulfilling one's ample expectations."

"You're beginning to sound like a professor in a law school," Kate said. "Something orotund has been added to your phrases."

"Only demonstrating my point about wonderful you."

"Not at all. I find it just as extraordinary that you should be a professor of law as that I should undertake a biography. All you're really saying is that yours was a sensible step into the unknown, and mine is less so. Admit it."

"All I'll admit is that I can't understand why you should be interested in that woman in the first place. All the women you know on a day-to-day basis who have settled down with writers to be their muse and do their washing strike you, at best, as having made an unwise, if possibly noble, choice."

"There aren't that many of them anymore. Women today who marry writers or live with them are usually writers themselves, or something equally demanding. You have to remember what Gabrielle was escaping from by running off with her handsome hero: the life of an upper-class English wife may have had a certain security, but it had damn little else. Her choices weren't that great; from what we know of her family after she ran off, they were practically nonexistent—her choices, I mean, not her family. She wanted excitement and challenge in her life, and she got it the only way she knew how. It is not fashionable these days to pity rich women—after all, they don't watch their children starve, or have to clean other women's kitchens—but they're a pretty powerless lot. I think it clever of Gabrielle to have grasped that.''

''Couldn't you say how clever it was in a short, pithy essay?''

''Perhaps. But there's more to Gabrielle than that. Everyone who has recently considered her seems convinced that she took some steps to counter her master's convictions and intentions. The memoir by Anne suggests that she may actually have written out these steps, but even if she didn't, even if the papers turn out to be a mare's nest, the hidden life of a woman of that generation requires looking into. That's my view. And I feel, somehow, given Simon's generous offer, inclined to look.''

''I knew you'd have it worked out to a fare-thee-well,'' Reed said proudly, like someone who has won a bet having backed a long shot. ''Where will you start?''

''I shall begin,'' Kate said in a manner pompous enough to amuse him, ''with a quotation from Luce Irigaray. Are you ready? 'Virgin means one as yet unmarked by men . . . not yet imprinted by their sex, their language.' ''

''Ah,'' Reed said. ''You're setting out to prove Gabrielle was all her life a virgin, said he brightly. And are you one too?''

"I knew you'd ask that, damn it," Kate said. "Of course I'm not. No member of an English department faculty is a virgin. Not yet, anyhow. Next question?"

Kate decided that it was only logical to begin her project by talking with Mark Hansford, whose biography of Emmanuel Foxx she had recently read. From Simon Pearlstine Kate had learned that Hansford was just past fifty, and had begun this work in the hope that it would be the capstone of an already distinguished career. Because of his reputation earned through his earlier biographies, he had been given a dignified advance against royalties, but (just between us, Pearlstine had said) the biography when produced had been rather a disappointment to its publisher and indeed generally. Kate knew little more of him than that.

Having informed him out of courtesy that she was doing the biography of Gabrielle, it was natural enough to mention her hope that she might talk with him, and her gratitude for any help that might be forthcoming. It was, in cold fact, in his interest to help her at least a little since the mention of one biography in another has a certain effect on the mentioned biography's reputation.

Rather to her surprise, however, he seemed remarkably reluctant to have a meeting, apprising her of this in a letter notable for its shortness if not exactly for its asperity. This was followed by a phone call in which he enlarged upon the letter and even, as he reported his mother used to say, let down his hair. "The fact is," he confided to her telephone receiver, "my wife and I almost broke up over Gabrielle. We're together again, and we've agreed to abandon her as a subject both between us or individually. If I can really help, call me at my office and we can talk on the phone or at least arrange a rendezvous. I'm sorry to be so circumspect, but marriage and research either mix very well or very badly. You wouldn't need to guess which it was in my case.''

Kate answered, with some astonishment, that she hadn't the smallest idea what he was talking about, and couldn't they at least meet long enough for her to ask him a few questions and let him know of her general intentions. Her tone implied, although she avoided saying any such thing, that she would be glad of the chance to speak of him in her forthcoming work, mentioning with gratitude his large-minded generosity as the best known of Emmanuel Foxx's biographers.

There was a silence during which Hansford apparently consulted his appointment book.

"I could meet you Thursday evening next week," he said. "My wife is going to one of Wagner's more long-winded operas, if that is not a comparison without meaning. How would that do?"

"Haven't I heard somewhere that *Das Rheingold* is a bit shorter?" Kate asked. "I share your emphatic uninterest in Wagner, so that could be the merest rumor. Thursday evening is just fine. May I buy you dinner first?"

"Thank you, but no thank you. I dine with my bride. I'll depart right after she does, and pray that she does not develop terminal Wagner indigestion on that particular evening. Can we meet at your house toward eight?" Kate, who felt as though she were working for the CIA, agreed.

He was there promptly at eight, and settled himself down with a drink and a faraway look that convinced Kate he had not only planned how to tell the story but perhaps even rehearsed it a little. He was, indeed, a rather self-satisfied man of a sort she recognized readily enough from long experience with male professorial colleagues. He could not imagine that his every word, even taking as long to expound as Wagner's lengthy efforts, would not be riveting. And in this case, Kate silently granted him, he was certainly right.

"I've asked around about you," Hansford said. "Of course I know your work. I gather you can be talked to as a woman of the world. I'm afraid you're going to need a great deal of sophistication for this story." Kate was inclined to guess that what she would need was a strong stomach, but, trying to look pleased at so manly a compliment, she placed the tray of ice, single-malt scotch, and macadamia nuts well within his reach and settled back to listen.

"Nineteen seventy-seven," Hansford began as though he were lecturing to a class, which in his imagination he probably was, or at least to a group of fascinated admirers, "was the Year of the Foxx, both in literary circles and spilling over into the popular press. Emmanuel Foxx had been dead twenty-five years, his masterpiece, *Ariadne*, had been (amazingly) published fifty years ago. People," Hansford smugly remarked, "feel a certain security in the presence of round numbers. Conferences on Foxx's oeuvre in general and *Ariadne* in particular were held in England, north and south, and in America from Toronto to Texas."

Kate nodded encouragingly. Her researches had revealed that attention at these conferences was neatly divided, as it had been since the publication of *Ariadne*, between male critics who considered Foxx a high modernist in the Pound, Eliot, Joyce tradition, and women who confronted him as the expounder of the female consciousness, whether limited to the male view of a female consciousness or considered to have surmounted the limitations of that male view to achieve true insight into the female mind and heart. There were women in the first camp (there are always women in the male camp), and some men in the women's camp (there are sometimes a few brave men discovered there). That the men in the women's camp were welcomed with more circumspection than the women in the men's camp simply reflected the habits of the powerful and the less powerful in the world at large. Kate, of course, maintained her fascinated gaze and said not a word of this.

"During the first decades after the publication of *Ariadne*," Hansford went on with no more than a pause in which to swallow and munch, "a number of scholars had attempted to interview Emmanuel's wife, Gabrielle. While she lived in Paris and then in London, she had turned them away, or bribed her landlady to do so. In 1955 she suffered something—a stroke, a heart attack, a brain hemorrhage— and was confined in a nursing home out of anyone's reach; it was rumored that not even her family, neither her granddaughter nor members of the family who were related to her through Emile's marriage, could get anything from her that could be called coherent speech. One diligent and remorseless scholar [of a type, Kate inferred, far inferior to Hansford], taking his cue from journalistic techniques, bribed his way into the nursing home to examine the files hoping to discover who had visited Gabrielle during the years she resided there."

Here Hansford rose to his feet and began pacing the living room, as no doubt he paced the front of the lecture room when he was teaching. His body language suggested that he had caught his audience with his story, and was adding an actor's drama to it. Kate, who never paced when teaching, watched him with serious, attentive mien.

"The only people, apart from those already known to have visited her," Hansford told Kate, representing in her single person an entire student audience, "were Anne Gringold, a longtime friend of Nellie, Gabrielle's granddaughter, and some nephew of Gabrielle's. The intruder had, in time, managed to get interviews with both of them, but had come away with so little information that he could not even write an article for a minor journal. It had soon become evident even to his blunted sensibilities that both the nephew and the granddaughter's friend had thrown up a most effective smoke screen, saying nothing while behaving like the most cooperative of interviewees."

Kate wondered how long it had been since he had had an audience as attentive, voluntary, and encouraging as she. Surely his students were often distracted from his antics. She watched, amused, as Hansford returned to the tray of drinks and refilled his glass while hardly pausing in his rendition.

"Five years earlier," Hansford went on, "anticipating the anniversary of Foxx's death, a major publisher commissioned from me a biography of the great writer, on very good terms, I might say. It would hardly be the first biography, but, it was assumed, one sufficiently monumental to be unchallenged for at least two decades. I don't know how much you know about the planning of biographies," he added as an aside, "though I'm sure you will learn if you haven't already, but the time required for research and writing always far exceeds the sanguine expectations of the publisher. In short: my biography was unlikely to be ready for this anniversary, and publishers, alas, are not the gentlemen they once were. Well, I was in a quandary, to put my condition at its mildest; the truth was, I was damn near beside myself with anxiety. For not only was I badly blocked, but my marriage had also begun to flounder. I don't know if you're a feminist," he added darkly, daring Kate to answer; she declined the opportunity, wanting information above all. Hansford seemed satisfied with her encouraging smile. "I won't say my wife is, but at this time she'd been reading too much feminist criticism. Anyway, her interpretation of my material, which she helped me to type in those days before everyone had computers, above all her theories about Foxx's masterpiece, *Ariadne*, brought our relationship to the brink."

Kate had no trouble interpreting this last remark. No doubt his wife's ideas, however much he had tried to attribute them to their failing personal relationship and her contamination by feminism, had badly shaken his faith in his own work.

"You mustn't think," Hansford said, "that I wasn't particularly diligent in my pursuit of those who had been acquainted with Emmanuel in his youth and during the years in Paris and in the other European cities." Kate had read enough to know of the many spots on the map of Europe where the Foxxes had, with great hopes, alighted, and from which they had, until settling in Paris, soon moved on. Yet even in Paris, they had exchanged one apartment for another with a rapidity that was startling, if less so in that time than in this. Hansford, she knew, had visited all these people, had indeed spent close to five years at that task alone, speaking to those who had known Foxx in his boyhood, in school, at Cambridge before he got himself rusticated, in England before his marriage.

"Of course," Hansford said, dropping onto the couch and gesturing toward Kate to emphasize his point, "I talked to the Goddards and I visited Dorinda." Here he paused to strengthen his drink and, Kate surmised, his nerve before launching into what she was beginning to guess was the crux of the matter. She remembered well enough that Dorinda's pictures had been the heart of the book Hansford had eventually produced.

"Rather to my surprise," Hansford said, launching himself into delicate matters, "Dorinda hardly seemed to begrudge me the time for long interviews. She showed me the pictures she had taken of Hilda, Emile, and Nellie. Most of the pictures of Nellie showed her with Anne Gringold, which further sharpened my sense of her importance and my annoyance at her refusal to talk to me."

Kate could guess at Hansford's frustration. Although he considered his interpretations of Foxx's works superior to any others, and although his interpretations benefited hugely from the advances in literary theory, feminist theory, deconstruction, and the like, he profoundly suspected that his biography of Emmanuel Foxx, so thoroughly researched and painstakingly written, was in fact not only old hat but a colossal bore.

"It was early in 1977," Hansford continued. "I find the holiday festivities of Christmas and New Year's, I'm sure not uniquely, depressing and conducive to marked irritability. It was just about this time that my editor became considerably less tolerant about my delays. This concatenation of the holidays and my editor's impatience catapulted me into a violent row with Judith, my wife." Kate interpreted this easily enough as well: Judith had told him that she was fed up with being his assistant, that she wanted to be his co-author, which role she fully deserved, and furthermore, she thought this biography dull, stupid, and uninspiring to say the least.

What Kate did not realize was that Judith had dropped a bombshell. "You will never guess what my wife said," Hansford added, unconsciously catching up with Kate's thoughts, and by now acting the part both of himself and of Judith. " 'What's more,' she said when, just before marching out of the bedroom and after announcing that she wanted, above all else, a separation for as long a time as possible, but probably forever, she stood at the front door in a stillness"—here Hansford assumed the pose of Judith as a statue—"remarkable after her stormy activities of renunciation, and announced that Emmanuel Foxx never wrote *Ariadne*, or at least that he didn't write all of it. 'Any woman could tell you that,' she actually said, 'but Foxx has been such a male domain, like Lawrence and Joyce and Pound, that no one's even bothered to analyze his writing!'

"Plenty of women have analyzed his writing, I shot back, as you can well imagine." And indeed Kate could. "Women, I told her, are always deciding whether to condemn Foxx for being a male chauvinist pig or to praise him for having remarkable insight into the female psyche. At any rate, they certainly admit that the central character is not only a woman but the best part of the book.

" 'They don't go far enough,' my wife insisted. She said that having spent so much time with this novel, not to mention his other works, that she was beginning to think she'd written it herself. That it was perfectly clear if Foxx didn't watch his wife, observe her, listen to women, imitate them, he stole their work, or at least, the work of one of them. She was very churned up at this point, as you can imagine. I pointed out that there was not one shred of evidence for such wild accusations, but she insisted that if there were, I would ridicule it as the sort of evidence that has harmless lunatics thinking that De Vere wrote Shakespeare and Shelley instead of his wife wrote *Frankenstein*.'' Hansford, having got sufficiently worked up himself, suddenly dropped back onto the couch and raised his glass as though he had been sitting there all along.

Kate murmured that she had gathered that Hansford's wife was very worked up.

''I assumed she was not, unless she had gone completely mad, going to suggest next that it was a female friend of Richardson's who wrote *Clarissa*.

''I quietly pointed out that literary examples were on my side. You won't believe this, but she actually insisted that it might have been. By now she was shouting about the way Lawrence used the words of women in *Sons and Lovers* and other books, at the way T. S. Eliot took his wife's very words and phrasing in *The Waste Land*, at how many professors' wives have written their husbands' books, or all but written them, and then been thanked profusely in the acknowledgments a year before the author divorced said wife and ran off with a graduate student!'' Hansford, who realized he had been rather carried away, stopped talking and began to fix himself a new drink.

Kate was amused to realize that it must have come to Hansford as a belated and unwelcome revelation that his wife had learned a good deal about modern British literature in the course of ''helping'' him with his books. The thought must have angered and frightened him.

''I don't mind telling you,'' Hansford said, ''that I started wondering whether or not she was about to claim she'd written my biography of Foxx."

Kate, who was beginning to get into the rhythm of his argument while bringing to it considerable knowledge of contemporary academic marriages, supposed that Judith had answered that she would hardly want to claim the writing of a biography so dull. But Hansford did not say so. What he did admit was that she had claimed everyone had already read all about Foxx's sexual exploits in previous biographies, and anyway, sexual exploits are less startling than they used to be, though no less exploitive.

"To tell you the truth," Hansford went on to confide in Kate, "I was rather hoping that my wife would get off on the emotional topic of sexual exploitation; it was one that was likely to engross her for some time." And, Kate silently added, perhaps lead her away from other, more sensitive topics, such as how disappointing his current work was, or how much of his three earlier biographies she had written. But Hansford admitted that Judith had declined, as she was increasingly declining, to meet his expectations. "She actually told me that she was thinking of trying to write a book of her own on 'my' marvelous Emmanuel Foxx. I was told to put that in my pipe and smoke it, after which the door slammed behind her."

Hansford rose from the couch and moved to a chair somewhat nearer to Kate. His posture became different, more relaxed and buddy-buddy: Kate gathered that she was now to be offered some manly details of sexual derring-do. She braced herself.

"Naturally," Hansford confided, "this did not increase my confidence but it did give me an idea, or at least the opportunity to follow through on an idea I'd been thinking about. Dorinda, you see, came to my mind offering hope. I wondered if I hadn't, after all, been rather impatient of her pictures, not the photographs themselves you understand, I didn't think of them at first, but her extremely detailed accounts of how and where each had been taken? She was, if one stopped to analyze it, a pivotal figure in the greater Foxx saga: friend of Nellie, niece of Hilda, cherished only child of the Goddards. There might well be a clue in her admittedly less than compelling anecdotes. My wife, Judith, always accused me of paying too little attention to women and the subjects of their speech. She once gave me a story to read by Susan Glaspell, 'A Jury of Her Peers,' which, frankly, I found annoying, though of course I praised it. I felt that Glaspell had carefully contrived the story to make her point: that men were fools and saw only what they were looking for.'' As though men did not ''contrive'' stories for their own ends, Kate thought, but did nothing to interrupt the by now torrential flow of his personal history.

"But, I thought," Hansford continued, "perhaps I should have taken the point more to heart. Might there be clues in Dorinda's admittedly rather extended narratives that I had overlooked? It seemed worth a try, anyway, and the time I interviewed her, she didn't make me feel that my presence was unwelcome. In fact, she invited me back.'' He grinned at Kate in a we-guys-understand-what-I-mean way. It was not the first time that Kate, as the object of a colleague's confidences, had found herself turned into one of the boys. Nor did she have any trouble reading Hansford's further thoughts: Dorinda was not the sort to attract him—she was older than he was—but the attention of a man, a professor and author, would not, he felt confident,

be rejected. And in some subtle way he chose not to analyze, such attentions would be getting back at Judith.

"Well," he continued in happy ignorance of Kate's
thoughts, "to my surprise Dorinda invited me to lunch at a
restaurant near where she worked; frankly, I hadn't been
aware that she worked at all. Somehow, I had imagined our
meeting in her living room, her plying me with tea, perhaps, or a drink, and something upper-class to eat, like
watercress sandwiches. Isn't it odd how we put people into
pigeonholes before we really know anything about them?"
He offered this bit of wisdom as though it were a break-
through in human thought. Well, Kate reminded herself,
he's about to tell me the tale of seducing Dorinda and he's
not quite sure how to go about it. Another drink, perhaps?
That always helps.

Kate sipped her soda water. She liked to drink, but only
in the right company and at what seemed to her appropriate
times. Since her ideas of the appropriate differed wildly
from most people's, her drinking habits were, as she had
often felt, ill understood. Hansford, sipping away, continued with his story, composed of occasional facts, frequent
innuendos, and a certain abashed satisfaction. Kate filled it
all in later for Reed.

"If you ask me," she told him when they were enjoying
their end-of-the-working-day drinks, "he was startled at her
picking a restaurant to meet in because he thought he might
be stuck with the bill. He's that sort of twit. As it turned
out, the restaurant she had chosen was one of those Italian
restaurants on the West Side where the food is excellent, the
tables small and crowded together, and the service somehow characteristically Italian in that the waiters spend more
time talking to each other and the barman than to the diners.

Hansford thought this might interfere with their confidences, but they stayed so long the restaurant emptied out. You remember, Reed: it must have been like that place on Columbus Avenue some lawyers took us to, where everyone was lining up to get into, with the good food and lousy service.''

Reed did remember, and commented on the fact that food badly served and eaten without the full benefits of leisurely conversation was hardly worth it; but, he reminded Kate, they were not gourmets, they were talkers, and maybe there was a generic difference. Anyway, Hansford wanted to talk, didn't he?

''I guess he did; they ended up with a bottle of wine, which he had to persuade her to drink since she was not in the habit of drinking in the afternoon. He actually quoted, he admitted to me, 'White wine eases the mind along,' unconscious at the time, as he ruefully confessed, that he was quoting a line from a woman poet Judith admired and who he had, at the time she read it to him, deprecated. Dorinda's response was, I was emphatically assured, all that he might have hoped.

''Hansford felt that she was getting into the spirit of the thing. He also reflected that she came from a very well-to-do family and might feel impelled to pay for the whole thing. The very rich, he assured me, lived in fear of being expected to pay for others, and always insisted on dividing checks, but the 'comfortable' were often generous, particularly in the company of academics. He was reassured to discover that Dorinda seemed to find him charming.

''He didn't even have to bring the conversation around to the Foxxes; she naturally supposed that was what he wanted to talk about, and she began to babble a good deal (his verb) about Emile, and Nellie, and Gabrielle. She reminded him that she had never met Emmanuel.''

Kate interrupted herself. ''The odd thing is,'' she told Reed, ''that I got a picture of Dorinda from his account. Oh, it's probably no help to the biography, but his descriptions of her were the only remarks he made that I couldn't have said for him without anyone noticing the substitution. He observed that she was one of those people who sipped her wine with deliberation, and infrequently, a habit that he detested. In addition, as though to confirm his direst expectations, she played with her bread, removing the soft center and molding it in her fingers until it became a series of dark, solid pellets. He had to restrain himself from removing the bread altogether from her reach. In an attempt to control his irritation he admired her fingernails. They were well within his gaze as his horror at her bread-molding seemed to keep his eyes riveted on her hands, as a rabbit is said to be transfixed by a snake.

''She was pleased with the compliment, apparently, and informed him with a certain complacency that she had ten moons, and always had had.

''You know, Reed,'' Kate interjected, ''I haven't heard anyone mention moons on fingernails since I was very young, and my mother taught me to be proud of *my* ten moons. Others, I gathered with that horrible youthful arrogance my mother did everything possible to encourage, had to push their cuticles back to reveal *their* moons, if any.''

''Are you telling me what you think happened—all right, what you *know* happened—or are you composing a cultural history of nails?''

"Am I boring you?" Kate curtly asked.

"You're not, but I think Hansford and Dorinda soon may. Did they say anything of use to you in your biographical endeavors?"

"They discussed Emile, whom I gather Dorinda never met. After he married her aunt, they came to the Jersey shore during several summers. Dorinda's father said it was clear the bloom had left the lily. Dorinda's grandfather, the sneaky one who tried to entice little girls on the Jersey shore, was going strong and that was why Hilda came with Emile, because her father adored his daughter and wanted to see her with the man she had married. I think the family found him rather a drip, as they used to say in Dorinda's day. Hansford gathered that he drank most of the time and was always impatient and bored. Dorinda's daddy said that was because he didn't have enough to do in life; being the son of a famous author was hardly a full-time occupation. He didn't even seem to care much about Nellie; they left her in Paris with her grandmother for that visit. Dorinda was only a baby, but she remembered very well their talking about it. She knew Nellie was her age, and, beloved only child that she was, couldn't imagine that anyone who had a child her age would go all the way across the ocean without it. Since Dorinda's mother hated to leave her, she thought Nellie's mother should feel the same and hate to leave her daughter, but that wasn't the case."

Kate smiled at Reed. "The fact is, Hansford's knowledge of the various family vicissitudes of the Foxxes was detailed enough so that he had no trouble understanding what Dorinda was talking about. But it was unclear if she could provide anything of use to a derailed biographer. He asked her if she had ever met Gabrielle, although he was pretty sure she hadn't. And of course," Kate added, "once he got onto Gabrielle I got out my recording skills, and remember exactly what he said she said; well, more or less."

"Which was?"

" 'No,' Dorinda told him, 'she didn't come to my wedding, although everyone tried to persuade her to come. My mother went to London to visit her in the nursing home, but by then she was gaga, or as close as made no difference. I was sorry; I've always had a kind of thing for Gabrielle.' "

" 'Thing?' Hansford asked.

" 'I mean,' Dorinda said, 'I always thought her story was so interesting, or would have been if anyone could have found out the details. I mean, she ran off with him when she was so young, and what can life have been for her, always in a strange city, with no family, probably no friends, losing her son and having to give up her grandchild? She was supposed to have been so beautiful, the typically beautiful English girl.'

"Here Hansford made a joke he was rather proud of, so he repeated it to me: 'with high coloring and low resistance,' Hansford said. It's the kind of thing he would say," Kate added. "Have you had enough of this?"

"Did Dorinda say anything else you've got by heart?"

"Yes, as a matter of fact. She said she imagined that Emmanuel Foxx when young was irresistible, one of those handsome, dashing men who carry their daimon with them, who crash through all the rules of boring, bourgeois existence and fear."

"I take it he saw that as the invitation it so clearly was," Reed said.

"All you men are the same," Kate muttered.

"Well, we all have functioning brains, if that's what you mean," Reed answered. "Or most of us."

"Well, you're right, of course. I suppose the semiotics of sexuality are rather clearly delineated."

"Get on with the damn seduction story, and spare me your theories of signifiers."

Kate laughed. "Well, Hansford suggested that such irresistible types as the Emmanuel Foxx she was describing cause immediate joy and lifelong suffering. He asked her if she didn't think Gabrielle had suffered.

" 'Of course she did,' Dorinda said. 'But at least she was part of something important. Something that mattered.' "

Reed winced. Kate ignored him. "Hansford asked if she really thought any novel, however celebrated, mattered that much. A strange question from a professor of literature, of course, but he was now on the road to sex with professional cares behind him. This was where he was a fool, needless to say, since the idiot might have found something more out about Gabrielle if he had kept his mind on his job."

"And what did Dorinda say, as though I couldn't guess."

"She said, as you have no doubt guessed, that she thought art mattered more than anything, and that to be able to create it, or to help someone create it, was a splendid destiny. Hansford pointed out that she hadn't married an artist. I gather Dorinda played further with her bread, rolling it into yet more dirty pellets until Hansford thought he would scream in agony; he said the worst part was there was no way to avert his eyes."

"But he didn't avert his eyes, and they ended up in bed. In his apartment?"

"So I gather. I think Dorinda's husband was in the habit

of dropping home from time to time, to refresh himself at the fount of domesticity, so she didn't like to chance it there.''

"This is beginning to sound like *Les Liaisons Dangereuses;* was a good time had by all?''

"Well, Hansford didn't go into details, to do him justice, but I did rather gather that she was trading the sex for the conversation; she seemed in rather a hurry.''

"I don't think she sounds a very promising person," Reed said.

"I'm not so sure. Remember, this was some years ago. That may have been her first foray into another possible life. Dorinda's probably twenty years older than I am, but in an odd way we grew up in the same conventional world. I think I understand her; I think I even sympathize. The next step, clearly, is to talk to her.''

"I gather they met again, and he got the photographs. Will you mention Hansford when you talk to her?''

"Not unless she does," Kate said. "And with any luck, I shan't have to see him again either. It doesn't take great skill to figure out that the dalliance with Dorinda may have provided excellent photographs for his book but did less than nothing for his marriage, nor that Judith had abandoned her Gabrielle project only as the price of a reconciliation. Mark, it was to be inferred, had similarly abandoned Dorinda, and had dedicated the tenth-anniversary edition of his biography to his wife.''

Four

DORINDA was, Kate felt confident, as emphatically through with Mark Hansford as he with her. Either she would never again speak about the Foxxes, or she would be relieved to speak about them with someone else. Why not, then, start with Dorinda? Kate felt a strong if unanalyzed inclination to undertake Anne only after her leave had really begun. Besides, a little discreet telephoning had revealed that Anne was at the moment abroad; Nellie was abroad, one understood less momentarily. Dorinda was right here in New York. As to the question of whether or not her relationship with Mark Hansford had soured her on the whole question of Emmanuel Foxx and his connections, one could only learn by asking. Kate decided not to write her request for a meeting; the little evidence she had suggested that Dorinda was likelier to be cooperative on impulse rather than on deeper thought or, worse, consultation with her husband. Husbands have a way of counseling caution; Kate did not yet know that this particular husband was caution personified.

Dorinda's response, upon being telephoned by Kate, was certainly abrupt: "If it's pictures you want, they've all been published; I really don't know what else I can tell you."

"Will you nonetheless be kind enough to meet and talk with me?" Kate asked. She hoped her voice didn't sound as plaintive as she feared; sorrowful requests were not Kate's mode. "I would be delighted to take you to lunch."

There was a long pause during which Dorinda was perhaps reflecting that lunch with a woman could hardly hold so many adventures and disappointments. It would be entirely beneficial for Kate to learn, in the not too distant future, that if she could read the mind of a mere male professor like Hansford, she was not half so clever when it came to Dorinda. Women who go to bed from time to time with less than clever men are not necessarily less than clever.

Dorinda agreed to the lunch; time, date, and place were settled. Kate immediately set to brooding about her questions. But it was hard to know what to ask a woman who had no doubt been asked everything before, was fed up with the subject of the Foxxes, and, like most unprofessional women of her generation, probably didn't see much point in talking to a woman anyway.

In this Kate, as she was soon to discover, did Dorinda an injustice. Dorinda might be over sixty, but she was not past the ability to undergo revelations. Still, impatience was certainly her prevailing note as she and Kate sat down to lunch. Since Kate had chosen the restaurant, it was devoted less to ethnicity than to graciousness, including widely spaced tables and unobtrusive waiters. Dorinda declined a drink, and immediately began to eviscerate the bread.

Remembering Anne's account of Dorinda, Kate was pleased to find that same theatrical, emphatic, finely hewn quality Anne had evoked still evident in the woman sitting across the table. The high cheekbones, the deeply sunken blue eyes, the fine, rather wild hair were there, palpable behind the wrinkles, the crow's feet, the drooping flesh above the eyes, almost, Kate thought, as though Dorinda were a young actress who had been made up to play herself as an old woman. Still slim, using her reading glasses as though they were a prop in a play, Dorinda astonished Kate with her double presence, simultaneously young and old, simultaneously stern and the same impulsive girl Anne had described.

Kate, judging her own mood with the most delicate of measurements, ordered one vodka martini with an olive: salt sharpened her senses. Dorinda, however, did not await Kate's introduction of her subject.

"So you want to write on Gabrielle; well, somebody ought to. I mean, perhaps it's time somebody stopped considering Emmanuel the world's best authority on women and looked into how he treated the women in his life. Do you know Mark Hansford?"

"Yes," Kate said, having flirted for the briefest moment with the possibility of, if not lying, shading the truth. "I can't say I thought him likely to become one of my favorite people."

"I threw myself at him, more or less," Dorinda flatly said. "I was just starting, at that time, to realize what kind of life I'd been buried in for all those years, and he was my first fling beyond its boundaries. It was a stupid thing to do;

I don't think it took me very long to figure that out. We met once again, to go over the pictures. I let him have them because it seemed to be separating me from my past. That was before I realized that I had two pasts, before my marriage and after. Anyway, if you talked to him, perhaps he told you that his wife wanted to write on Gabrielle. I gather she gave it up when Mark returned to the fold. I thought then and I think now it's a damn good idea. What made you think of it?''

"A publisher thought of it," Kate said. "He offered me a contract. I was intrigued."

"Why start with me?"

"You're here in New York. But the main reason was your wonderful pictures. There must be some story behind those pictures."

"Mark didn't think so. He just wanted the pictures."

"His book didn't say what camera you used."

"A Leica. I've got a new one now. But I've always preferred a range-finder camera, particularly for portraits. My husband has one of those single-lens reflex jobs that sets the aperture and speed, in fact everything but the focus, and it will do that if you just want a sweeping scene. I'm not putting those cameras down; they just don't interest me. Perhaps it's nostalgia. I got my first Leica when I was twelve, from German refugees, an M-three. I still have it. So, I think, does Anne."

Kate, who was, looked impressed and questioning.

"My father was given two, actually, and he gave one to Anne. I think she still has it; at least, she had it a while ago and said she would never willingly part with it. Did you really want to talk about cameras?"

But Kate faced a harder question than that. Ought she to

mention Anne's memoir? Simon Pearlstine had put no restrictions upon her, but might not Dorinda resent that memoir, or even the fact of its having been written? She would not have to be a saint to feel that Anne had usurped her experience, her life. Dorinda, as Kate would soon discover was her wont, said the unexpected.

"Have you read the essay Anne wrote on our childhood, or was that sent to a different publisher?"

"I have read it. That memoir was part of the reason the publisher decided upon a biography of Gabrielle. Yet in a way, it was more a biography of you and Anne. What a wonderful childhood."

"Do you really think so?" Dorinda asked, and looked at Kate as though actually awaiting, interested in, her answer. Dorinda was turning out rather differently than Kate had expected, a fact in which Kate silently rejoiced. She particularly admired people whose every opinion was not predictable.

"No," Kate said. "Not really. It's considered bad form to complain about wealthy childhoods, and I can understand why. If I had not had one, I would certainly think that anyone unhappy under those conditions was a fool."

"As Heathcliff says about the Lintons in *Wuthering Heights*. I understand you're a professor of English literature."

"Where did you pick up that understanding?" Kate asked. She had said nothing about herself on the telephone.

"I do research," was Dorinda's only rather enigmatic answer.

"Well," Kate said, recovering herself, "you're certainly right about Heathcliff. Who would rather be a Linton, except, of course, everybody who hasn't been? Certainly not Cathy."

There was a perceptible pause. Kate was occupied with readjusting her assumptions, a task as welcome as it was difficult. She hoped she would not have to fill in the silence with meaningless chatter, but was gearing herself for this unpleasant task (Virginia Woolf had called it beating up the waves of conversation) when Dorinda spoke. She had apparently decided to fill Kate in on the facts. "As you probably already know, I never met Emmanuel or Gabrielle, but I heard about them so much from Hilda and my father, and later from Nellie, that I felt I knew them. My mother went over to visit Gabrielle in her last years in the nursing home, but she was really out of it by then, so there wasn't much more to learn. But I feel I was there, with my mother, after hearing her description. Gabrielle would suddenly wake up and it seemed to Mummy that she would start up, frightened, and then remember something satisfactory, and sink back with the smallest of smiles, as though it had come back to her that everything was okay, it was taken care of."

"What was 'it'?"

"I don't know. There may not have been anything. But Mummy is very good at re-creating scenes, at making you see them. I suppose it comes from living with the Goddards and putting up with the scenes only by describing them later. Goddard scenes were always wild."

"They aren't anymore?"

"No. Grandpa died. Then Hilda. Then Daddy. There's only Mummy and me left. She approves of my life, which was the sort I think she always wanted, but sometimes we sit around and remember and laugh. Just the other day she described how every time she got a workman in to do some needed repair, if she didn't warn Daddy and plead with him not to interfere, he would come across the man doing his work and shout questions and suggestions at him at the top of his voice, his normal way of speaking, of course, so that inevitably the workman would put down his tools and stomp out. Mummy always had to plead with the workman to come back and explain, in the nicest possible way, that her husband was a harmless lunatic.''

"But I gather his devotion to his sister was extreme, especially when she married Emile Foxx."

"It was always extreme. Hilda was the apple of her father's and her brother's eye—does anyone use that expression anymore? They worried about her when she married Emile, but secretly I think they thought it very clever of her to bring such a famous writer into the family. I used to think so myself."

Kate nodded her comprehension of the change of mind Dorinda suggested.

"Lately, I've thought a good deal about Gabrielle. Mostly because I began recently to think about my mother. I mean *really* think. She saw Gabrielle as often as anyone still living. You ought to try to talk with her."

"What is it you research?" Kate asked because suddenly she really wanted to know.

"I work in a hospital lab. My husband helped me to get the job, and I turned out to be rather good at it. I'm interested in medicine, which is probably what I saw in him in the first place." Dorinda paused. "Tell me, does everyone say things to you they didn't even know they thought, let alone thought of saying?"

"I suspect I just came along at the right time. What do you do in the hospital, exactly?"

"Someone has a fever, who knows why? Not the doctors, who find that their antibiotics won't bring it down; they have to resort to wet sheets, as though it were a century ago. But, aha! They do have technological advances at their disposal! So, they drill into the poor man, get out a little round section of his liver, and bring it down for me to do things with."

"You make it sound sinister."

"It is, more times than not. Some guy is doing a paper on livers. He needs samples. He takes them, even when they can be fairly sure that the liver is not responsible. Have to have enough data for one's paper. Often the patients are poor or ignorant and can't object, but even rich patients have to take the doctor's word for everything. But don't let me sound too cynical; the fact is, I like looking at livers and other bits and pieces. I should have been a doctor, not the kind that helps people, but the kind who tries to find out what started an epidemic, that sort of thing. You're easy to talk to. Or perhaps I just need to talk. And don't tell me I should see a psychiatrist. That's what Arthur keeps saying when I mention that I might like to talk to him about our life. Arthur's my husband, a brain surgeon. He's a little less skilled at what's in brains he isn't cutting up."

"Which is why Mark Hansford was a sort of trial run away from Arthur?" Kate asked.

"A pretty sad trial run. I guess I knew he wasn't going to be any better at listening than Arthur. Do you think men were born without some essential equipment for listening when they aren't paid for it, and even sometimes when they are? Do you imagine Gabrielle thought the same thing? I know the prevailing opinion is that Emmanuel got all he knew about women by listening to her, but doesn't that come under the heading of being paid for it?''

Kate decided to latch on to the only subject about which she could inquire without seeming to probe. Women may know how to listen, but few individuals of either sex know how to demonstrate interest as opposed to curiosity. In any case, questions were rarely the way to manifest genuine interest.

''I'd like to hear more about your mother,'' Kate said. ''Anne obviously liked her; she seemed to have a rough row to hoe.''

''More like sailing into the wind, I should have said. Oh, my father was fascinating in his way. I thought him wonderful because, like his sister Hilda, I was truly loved by him. But he could be devastating. I remember once his telling Nellie at the beach club that he'd got bigger breasts than she. It was true, of course; Nellie had tiny little breasts, and my father was rather fat. But it wasn't the sort of thing a sensitive man said to an adolescent girl. Anne and I both felt bad for her, though Anne said she wished she had breasts like Nellie's, and I think Nellie believed her. My father wasn't easy on my mother. He just went around being noble to people like the Foxxes and left my mother to cope with the results. And she did cope, beautifully. My aunt Hilda scorned her; so did I, until quite recently. She wasn't a glamorous person. I think the only person she ever brought into the household was Anne; perhaps she sensed a potential ally, someone like herself.''

''You all seem to have been so marvelously generous,'' Kate said. ''Anne clearly thought so.''

''With reservations,'' Dorinda said. ''I've read that memoir. She sent it to me, as was only decent of her. Anne is always decent. I know that sounds condescending, but I don't mean it to. I've come to admire decency more than I used to. I used to call it values. But today one can't help noticing the people who talk most about values tend to get involved in the most steamy scandals. That's what I'd call Anne: decent. And she was right to say that our generosity cost us little. She gave as much as she got, like most adopted children.''

"That doesn't change the fact that you treated her and Nellie well, and somehow never lost either of them. I think that's worthy of quite a tribute.''

"Maybe. I credit my mother with most of that. Oh, I liked playing Lady Bountiful when I was young; until rather recently, in fact. I was playing Lady Bountiful with Mark Hansford.''

Kate suddenly remembered a time in her youth, though she could not remember where it was, when she had put a quarter into one of those gambling machines and been rewarded with so many quarters she needed help in gathering them up; she remembered not knowing where to put them, how to carry them, until a kind woman gave her a brown paper bag.

"Do you think I might call your mother and ask her to talk with me?" Kate asked.

"Do you know something about you that is most unusual? I've taken to noticing this, so I might as well mention it. You don't ask questions unless you really want to know the answer. Arthur asks questions all the time, it's his only means of discourse—conversation I will not call it—and he never listens to the answers. I told that to Mark Hansford before I realized he was exactly the same way. About my

111

mother, do call her. I'll give you her number, and tell her to expect a call. She was probably the last person to see Gabrielle, and she certainly had the most objective view of Nellie; also, I suspect that Nellie talked to her about things she didn't mention to Anne and me, though I've only recently come to realize that.''

"She must be old, as Master Shallow said to Falstaff,'' Kate remarked, feeling skittish.

"She's ninety-two, but you'll find she can talk to you about the Foxxes, all right. She's very clear on the old days. It's the immediate past and the present about which she gets a little fuzzy and forgetful. She's a nice person; always was.''

"I hope that doesn't mean you won't talk to me anymore yourself."

"I'll be glad to talk to you," Dorinda said. "I've found when one begins to remember, one remembers more than one knew. Proust and all that: you can only really remember what you've forgotten. But for me, Emmanuel Foxx was a glamorous figure; I liked to have fantasies, if you can believe it, about being the last woman in his life to inspire him. I never told Nellie that, of course. Nellie's the one who really loved Gabrielle, but, as with so many families, only when she was away from her. You must talk to Nellie. I'll help you. I'd like to help you. Shall I tell you something awful? I read recently about a number of women, all gifted, if not geniuses they were remarkably talented, who took up with young men in their old age. And I learned something from that. I've begun collecting these women, I've got four so far. It isn't just that old men are still sexy and old women are not, as I always thought. It's that old men have power. And when old women have it, they become sexy too. Sexy is just another word for clout once you're past forty.''

"You're right," Kate said. "I've noticed it too.''

"You mean you've always known it. Let me tell you all the other facts about me." She held up her hand, prepared to raise one finger for each fact. "I like medical research. I learn from thinking about the past. I have four sons, which is one less than Sally Seton, but I do not grow blue hydrangeas or flowers of any other color. Otherwise, Lady Rosseter and I have a lot in common. I have a husband to whom I have not really talked in at least twenty years; if the CIA were to overhear one of our phone conversations, they'd be certain we were speaking in code, there being no other rational explanation for such an impersonal exchange." She dropped her hand. "Five facts. I like talking to you. Let me pay for the lunch. I know, you invited me, but you can pay next time when I promise to answer all your questions about Gabrielle. I like your questions.''

And Kate agreed, knowing there are some things we must pay for because it feels, at that moment, like the right thing to do.

"Who's Sally Seton when she's at home, as you have told me Molly Bloom put it?" Reed asked that evening. They were sipping single-malt scotch and relating the events of their day. Reed's day had offered more frustrations than events, the number of the former being responsible for the lack of the latter, and he was glad to forget it and hear about Dorinda and Sally Seton.

"Sally Seton is a character in a novel by Virginia Woolf called *Mrs. Dalloway*," Kate said. "She is wild and wonderful in her youth, and turns into a dreadful lady who lives a life of aching rectitude and propriety. What's interesting is not only that Dorinda so characterizes herself but that Anne mentioned Sally Seton also in her memoir. They must have read that novel together while they were reading Elizabeth Bowen."

"Of whom I have heard. Lived longer than Woolf."

"Correct, oh you dear man who listens. I never thought about what an unusual man you are in that respect until Dorinda mentioned it, indirectly of course."

"I am unusual in every respect, as I thought you knew."

"Not least of all in putting up with me." They both laughed, having had a version of this conversation many times before.

"Going to see Dorinda's mother soon?" Reed asked by the time they were onto their second drink.

"Certainly. Although talking to a ninety-two-year-old woman may be rather uphill work. Still, maybe she will surprise me; Dorinda did. Is there a greater joy than watching people you've pegged become unpegged? Do you know the most surprising thing about Dorinda, among so many surprises? Rhetorical questions, no response required. She must have realized I had read in Anne's memoir about her wild youth. Her mentioning Sally Seton told me that. And yet, she has decided to trust me. I have a feeling she hasn't trusted many people lately. Perhaps if one can begin to trust one's mother in one's sixties, one is ready for anything."

"Unless," Reed said, "one is sufficiently lucky never to be given the chance. Not all mothers are redeemable."

"Alas, how true. I must not be carried away, as you so wisely suggest, by some totally unwarranted belief in the possibilities of human nature."

"One is carried away," Reed said sternly, "when one drinks single-malt scotch: that is one of its beautiful qualities."

Eleanor Goddard, at ninety-two, lived in half of the apartment the Goddards had occupied in the old days. The landlord, while the building was still a rental and not a co-op, had persuaded her to abandon the back half of her nine rooms. This left her a huge living room without the Capehart, a dining room, a large bedroom, and a smaller bedroom for her companion, plus two and a half bathrooms. She preferred, she told Kate, not to speculate about what price the landlord had got for the back part of her apartment.

Eleanor, as Kate was asked to call her, was elegantly dressed and sitting in the living room when Kate was introduced by someone pleasant in a white uniform. They were soon left alone, and Kate had barely seated herself before she was assured that Dorinda had called about her, and that she, Eleanor, would be happy to talk about the Foxxes or anyone else.

"There aren't many people who ask for the privilege of listening to the memories of a very old lady. I remember Pop, as we called Sig's father, rambling on endlessly and I swore when I was old I would never talk about anything past unless specifically asked. Believe me, it is nice to be asked. Can I offer you something, tea, a drink, a soft drink?"

"I'm just fine," Kate said. "Unless you want something. I'm happy just to talk and listen."

"Lovely. I wonder what you made of Dorinda. How did she impress you?"

"I was hoping to be the one asking questions," Kate said, smiling. "I liked Dorinda. I had the distinct impression that she is reconsidering her life, which is, on the whole, a good thing to do.''

"On the whole?"

Kate marveled that she had found the sharpest old lady in the universe. Would she answer questions as neatly as she asked them? "Many people I know," Kate said, "most of them relatives and family friends, reconsider their lives only as a way to replay old injuries, old ways in which life did them dirt. I had the sense from Dorinda that she was reconsidering for the future, not to belabor the past."

"I'm glad to hear it. Dorinda has always been a puzzle to me; I admit it freely. Even as a baby, she and I never seemed to be in touch. We had another girl living with us named Anne, and she was the sort of child I would have expected to have. She's been closer to me than Dorinda, if truth be told, and when you're ninety-two you're either telling the truth or the same old stories unchanged. Odd to only begin really talking to your daughter when she's over sixty and you're older than God, as Sig used to say.

"The problem, really, was Dorinda's marriage. I could never understand why she married Arthur. Well, the truth is, I could never understand anything about Dorinda, but her marriage least of all. It always reminded me of that old story about the most beautiful woman in London who married the dullest man in England. When asked why, she said it was the only way she could be certain of never again having to sit next to him at dinner. But that hardly seems motive enough for Dorinda. You came to talk about Gabrielle Foxx, and here I am babbling on about my daughter."

"I gather from Dorinda that your husband was far from the dullest man anywhere."

"No one could call Sig dull," Eleanor agreed. "No,

THE PLAYERS COME AGAIN

there is no way anyone could call him that. He plucked me out of a lower-middle-class world, working-class really, where we always tried to pretend we had more than we did. Sig and the Goddards and all their friends never pretended that; I used to think because it wasn't possible to have more than they did, so why pretend?" She chuckled. "They were Jews, you know, which meant they lacked that essential dullness that does rather mark Anglo-Saxons. I remember during the war, World War II I mean, Sig and his family did a lot to rescue Jews from Germany and Austria and other countries. Some of these Jewish families had been rich themselves, in Europe. When they came here, they all complained endlessly about America and about how much better everything was in the old country. Sig was far more tolerant of that than I. But what," she said, shaking her head, "has that to do with anything. Forgive me, my dear. Everyone I used to know is dead. And even when I read about some old person who has done or said something, she is always younger than I am, though sometimes not much. I am a relic. You must keep me on the Foxxes and ask your questions."

"All of this is important to my work, and interesting besides. Honestly. Did you get the name Dorinda from Ellen Glasgow?"

"Yes I did, dear. Oh, clever of you! Everyone else assumed I made it up to be fancy; I said I liked the name and that was that. Sig would only have cared about a son's name. The truth is, I read *Barren Ground* while I was pregnant with Dorinda; it had just come out. I don't know why that novel affected me as it did. I think I hoped my daughter would have Dorinda's courage. She had so much when she was young, and so little later, my Dorinda, I mean. But perhaps that is changing. Have you met Arthur?''

Kate shook her head. ''It's a fate best avoided,'' Eleanor said. ''I tried to think that even bores are interesting because they're bores. There has got to be something interesting about everyone, if you don't see them too often. That was a nice thought, but Arthur defeated it.''

''Maybe you saw him too often?''

''Not really. He was always at the hospital, or playing golf, or somewhere else. But if he did come home, you could feel the temperature of the room drop, as though someone had splashed cold water around. I never liked Arthur, and the remarkable thing is, he is the first person I ever admitted not liking. It was a great relief. But it didn't do much to bring Dorinda and me closer.'' She paused, as though, Kate thought, in amazement at how much she had said. She looked expectantly at Kate.

''How often did you see Gabrielle?'' Kate asked.

''Let me see. I first saw her when Hilda decided to marry Emile. Sig and I sailed, on the *Ile de France* I think it was, but we crossed the ocean often and I may have the wrong ship. Travel was a joy in those days. It was clear that Gabrielle was not at all pleased with the marriage, and I didn't blame her. We tended to talk while everyone else was dancing attendance on Emmanuel, and I knew how she felt. I think we both realized that Emile was a substitute-Emmanuel for Hilda, her way into the exciting world of Paris writers, and, understandably, Gabrielle wanted someone to love Emile for himself.

''Gabrielle kindly took me for short walks in Paris; our absence was hardly noticed, certainly not by anyone but Emmanuel who would suddenly want something, discover she wasn't there, and insist she must be found at once. I think she was a kind of talisman for him, something he felt lost without. Everyone would come rushing to search us out—we were always sitting in a café not far off—and Gabrielle would have to go back. I sometimes felt we were mysteriously on the edge of a real conversation, but it never happened. Perhaps if I had stayed on longer, it would have, but that's probably an old woman's memory filtered through rose-colored glasses. Are you sure you won't have something to drink, or some tea?''

"Quite sure," Kate said. "When was the next time you saw her?"

"My goodness; there hasn't been anyone hanging on my every word since—well, perhaps no one ever hung on my words; Anne, maybe. Certainly neither Sig nor Dorinda did. I saw Gabrielle a few times when we were in Europe before the war. When Emmanuel died, the war was on and it wasn't possible to go to Gabrielle; Sig got Hilda out just in the nick of time; she was in a rest home; Emile had left her. Nellie, their daughter, was living with Gabrielle, and we brought her, Nellie, over to America. I guess you know all that. I often think back at the cruelty of our taking away the last person Gabrielle had left, but of course we were all just thinking of the girl. She was exactly Dorinda's age and dying to come to America and live with us. We are often so cruel without meaning it, as though that were an excuse. I try to tell myself Nellie might have been killed, but that's hardly the point."

These last words were said in a slow, drawling manner, and Kate saw that Eleanor had dozed off; her head dropped slightly to one side; her eyes were closed. Kate sat watching her for quite a while, marveling at the woman. After a time, the attendant in white came in and spoke softly to Kate.

119

"She hasn't talked that long since I've been here, and that's seven years. She'll sleep a while now. It doesn't mean she wasn't glad to see you; it's her age, you know."

"Do you think I can come again?" Kate said. "Have I worn her out?"

"She's loved it; you come again anytime. But do call first; some days are better than others. I think you've done her a world of good."

"And she me," Kate said, walking from the room, her footsteps silent on the thick carpet.

Five

"ARIADNE, in mythology, daughter of Minos (q.v.) and Pasiphaë. When Theseus (q.v.) came to Crete, she fell in love with him and gave him a clue of thread by which he found his way out of the Labyrinth after killing the Minotaur. He then fled, taking her with him, but (magically?) forgot and left her on Naxos (Dia). It is generally said that Dionysus found her there and married her. . . ."

—*The Oxford Classical Dictionary*, 2nd Edition

"Matrilinear custom deprived an heiress of all claims to her lands if she accompanied a husband overseas; and this explains why Theseus did not bring Ariadne back to Athens, or any further than Dia, a Cretan island within sight of Cnossus. . . ."

—*The Greek Myths*, Robert Graves

FROM her earliest memories, Sundays had been trying days for Kate. She still claimed that, should she wake from a coma, she would know if it were Sunday. Perhaps it was that families were together on Sunday, stayed at home

121

and pretended, if they were adults, to enjoy this "family" day. Kate could still sense her father's noisy silence, her mother's irritation, the haste with which, after the awful midday family dinner, her brothers found reasons to leave the house if, indeed, they were not old enough to have already escaped being there at all. Those times were long passed, but little even now could remove the sticky stigma of Sunday and its endless, unmoving hours. The only strategy that Kate had developed over the years was to make it a working day, on a far stricter and more demanding scale than other days when time seemed capable of organizing itself in reasonable and reliable ways. She arose earlier than usual, spent a half hour with the fat Sunday newspaper which she would pick up in casual moments during the week, and got down to serious work, meticulously planned the night before. This scheme, faithfully adhered to, not only passed the day but brought the evening in with less of a sense of dread, a dread which, even in her earliest years, the promise of evening radio programs had not been sufficient to assuage.

Her work for this Sunday was a serious contemplation of *Ariadne* by Foxx, a novel whose rereading she had just completed. In keeping with the habits of modernist writers, Foxx had not presented his readers with the story of Ariadne in any of its mythic forms; he either assumed knowledge on the part of his readers, or ignored its necessity. (T. S. Eliot's notes for *The Waste Land*, the only apparent exception to this generality, had, as any English graduate student knew, been added by him to fill up extra pages in the poem's original binding and were wonderfully insufficient to an understanding of that poem's sources.) The title, however, for Foxx as for Joyce, whispered the necessary clue. All modernist writers were fascinated by the figure of the labyrinth and the Minotaur Daedalus had hidden there, but none before Foxx had made Ariadne the center of his tale. Women writers of that period apparently preferred, as Kate reflected, to create their own female heroes, leaving those of mythology to the men. And the men had, for the most part, ignored the women or exiled them to their separate chapters or sections. Only Foxx had decided to put his woman in the middle, to make her consciousness the center of his masterpiece.

The book began as Ariadne and her court awaited the arrival of the bull leapers from across the sea. She had forewarning that Theseus would be among them, and that she would love him. What that love would mean was the question she posed for herself in the early part of Foxx's novel. Her mother, Pasiphaë, had loved a bull, and Daedalus had contrived for her the form of cow inside of which she might allow the bull to satisfy her passion. The Minotaur, born of this union, was hidden at the heart of the labyrinth, and Ariadne was destined to love the man who killed him and was able to find his way out of the labyrinth—for that was the hard part. Because she was a priestess, and because the educated reader already knew it or could find out by reading one of the many books explaining his novel, Foxx allowed Ariadne awareness of the other (future) fatal love in her family, that of Ariadne's sister Phaedre for her stepson, Hippolytus, the child of Theseus and Hippolyta, queen of the Amazons, whom Theseus had defeated in battle. Fatal loves were clearly the curse on that family, and it was Foxx's fascination with these fatal loves, with the fatal loves of all women, that formed the heart of his novel. And, Kate reflected, Ariadne's violent and instantaneous passion for Theseus was one for which Foxx had the perfect model in Gabrielle's similar desire, indeed lust, for himself.

That Ariadne, by providing Theseus with the thread for the labyrinth, had made inevitable her own sad destiny was an irony not lost on Foxx. So, he thought, all women contrived their own passions, and all men used them for their own ends. If a woman considers herself destined to love— and what woman does not, Foxx would have asked—she will provide the required condition of her passion, if, of course, she is in a position to control any part of her life. The wonder for Foxx of Ariadne's actions was that, living in a matriarchy and having within her grasp enormous powers as a priestess and queen, she had offered her power to a man whose choice or fate it would be to desert her. That the established accounts of her affair with Theseus should mention prominently her father and her lover (for readers were not urged to "q.v.," that is go "see" any account of Pasiphaë, Ariadne's mother, or any other woman) indicated the male side of this story that all recorded history had emphasized. Women longed to help men, to be loved by them, to be carried off to ancillary destinies; this much Foxx knew. But he dared to tell that story from the woman's point of view. That Ariadne had gone no farther than the island of Dia might, according to Graves, be because she did not wish to lose her claims to her lands, but Foxx believed, as his novel made evident, that Theseus had deserted her because her powers frightened him, or because he recognized Dionysus as having a greater right to Ariadne.

Kate was greatly impressed with Foxx's self-admiration when she realized that he had combined Theseus and Dionysus into one character, Ariadne's chief lover. The character Ariadne in Foxx's novel was called Artemisia, the name given to Foxx's granddaughter, but, in the case of the granddaughter (as Kate had learned from Anne's memoir) immediately abandoned for "Nellie." Picking up the most obvious strands from biographies of Foxx, Hansford's and others', Kate guessed that Gabrielle had led Foxx at the time of their first meeting through labyrinthlike paths to the beech tree grove where she had become his lover, his willing slave. According to the legends Kate had recently re-read, Dionysus had transformed Ariadne into a goddess, or a star, and clearly Foxx saw himself as having performed the same task for Gabrielle. The question remained: where was the real woman Gabrielle in all this, at the center as Foxx claimed, or only at the center of her creator's imagination and therefore secondary to him?

By the time Kate had sorted all this out, her Sunday was largely conquered, and she was ready in the evening to join Reed in outraged contemplation of the current events described in the Sunday newspaper. But why, she continued to ponder, had Foxx made Artemisia's lovers either inadequate men or women?

For Artemisia had not ceased her lovemaking with the Theseus figure; she had gone on to other loves and other passions, some with feeble men, lacking either physical or mental prowess, or, in one extraordinary scene, to a passionate encounter with another woman. Unlike D. H. Lawrence, whose enactment of a lesbian love had rendered it sinister and life-demeaning, Foxx had shown the passion of the two women in a fulfilling, almost magical light. In the end, his heroine's woman lover, like Lawrence's, had abandoned the love of women for the love of an evil man, but while her passion for Artemisia lasted it provided the heart of the book, as well as the primary reason for its censorship.

Artemisia had doubted the wonder of men, but, unlike Joyce's Molly Bloom, she did not despise other women. It was this fact that had prevented Foxx's masculine-centered book from being wholly dismissed by women through the years of feminist criticism in the seventies and eighties. No wonder there had been questions about Gabrielle; no wonder, Kate thought, that the discovery of Anne's memoir had at last opened the possibility of a biography of her.

What could Gabrielle possibly have made of *Ariadne*? Damn it, why did you die? Kate found herself irrationally addressing Gabrielle; why didn't you tell us what you thought? Why didn't you at least tell Nellie, or Anne? Did you indeed write it all down and leave it to Anne to hide away?

In all the biographies of Foxx there had been reports from people who had spoken to Gabrielle, who, friends of both the author and his wife, had reported comments of Gabrielle's made in passing, or confided in an off moment. She had told one man that her husband had encouraged her love affairs with other men because he wished to study her responses to them. Could that possibly be true, and if true, did Gabrielle follow through on the request? Kate had begged from Dorinda a copy of the picture of Gabrielle at the window and had hung it above her desk. It seemed to claim her attention in a supernatural way.

"Turn around," Kate wanted to say, did say; "tell me what you are thinking, what you make of all this brouhaha about a book that you must understand better than anyone."

Would Gabrielle have been likely to tell anyone of the cruelties, if there were cruelties, in her marriage? She was a proud woman; on that all who knew her agreed. She had been scorned by her family, and scorned them and all the

English aristocracy in her turn. But the pride of caste is hard to shake off; certainly the habit of it clings long after belief in its justification has been shaken. Could such a woman have said: "He wants me to go with other men"?

Had she returned to England in an attempt to reclaim England, as Ariadne may have stayed on Dia to reclaim her inheritance? But Cnossus was a matriarchy, which no one in her right mind could accuse England of being. Why, after all, had Gabrielle returned to England? Well, why not? It was her first home.

Kate gave the dreary news of the world as she and Reed discussed it only part of her mind, as he was quick to notice.

"Gabrielle seems to have claimed you," he said. "But what I can't decide is whether you are engaged as a detective or as a scholar and writer."

"I haven't a clue," Kate said. "If you want a definition of our time, there it is: there are no longer any clues to the labyrinth, not for love, and not for power."

"For what, then?" Reed asked.

"One must find the thread for oneself, now that Ariadne has given us the hint. Simple, really."

And they laughed at that.

By the following week Kate had made up her mind that Nellie was the next one to be interviewed. It turned out that she was in Switzerland, working for an international organization that required languages and a dedication to causes beyond nationalism. Kate wrote to her, forming the letter with care, suggesting that she wished to meet her, to write of her grandmother, but that she would respect any of Nellie's wishes not to be quoted or not to be asked about certain things. Kate provided her own academic qualifications and assurances from the publisher as well as herself that this biography of Gabrielle would be as sound, as unspectacular, and as unjournalistic as could possibly be hoped.

The response to this carefully contrived letter was short and disturbing, if not, Kate had to admit, rude. Nellie Foxx—she signed herself by that name which she had apparently made legally hers—appreciated Kate's honorable intentions and her outstanding qualifications for writing the biography. She had, however, long ago become convinced that the dead had a right to their privacy, that consequently Gabrielle's relationship to Emmanuel Foxx did not permit the betrayal of her personal papers. She had therefore burned all her letters from Gabrielle and all the other letters from Gabrielle she had been able to acquire. So she could not produce any letters for Kate's or anyone else's use, as she hoped would become widely known. If, however, Kate found herself in Geneva, Nellie would be happy to meet with her to indicate that there was nothing personal about her position in this matter, and that her decision to burn the letters was not to be perceived as in any way discourteous to Kate, but rather as a matter of principle. The letters had, in any case, been burned years ago. Furthermore, she would be glad to assist Kate in any way if she could. And she was very truly Kate's.

Horrified, Kate called Simon Pearlstine to ask—demand would more properly describe her tone—if he had known about Nellie's burning of Gabrielle's papers.

"It had been rumored, certainly," Simon answered. "But we had all hoped that it was not true. Nellie has very emphatic views on this, that everyone knew, but no one knew she'd actually done it. I think you should take it as a good sign that she has written to you so frankly and offered to talk with you; that looks like quite a compliment to me."

"I'd rather she'd kept the letters and refused to talk to me, if you want to know," Kate shot back.

"But that wouldn't necessarily have helped you. She could still have refused to let you see the papers, let alone publish them. It isn't as though she'd put them in a library somewhere, or sold them. I think talking with her may be more productive."

"I feel you have tried to put something over on me, frankly," Kate said. "I don't know that I'd have taken this on if I'd been aware that most if not all of Gabrielle's letters had been destroyed."

"At least you know for sure," Simon maddeningly replied. "So far, it's only been rumored. Why not go off to Geneva and save your recriminations until you return. At least spend some of the advance before you decide to return it and abandon so fascinating a project."

"I was wrong about you," Kate said. "You're no different from other publishers: money, money, money."

"Let's have a good lunch complete with wine when you get back," Simon said. Kate did not exactly hang up on him, but she didn't exactly say good-bye either. She just replaced the receiver slowly, contemplating Geneva.

Six

THAT evening Kate asked Reed if he happened to have a map of Geneva. She could, of course, have walked to the nearest bookstore and bought the newest guidebook, but generosity and the secret love we have for those who refuse to adopt our efficiencies required that she ask Reed if he had such a map. Kate believed that in enduring marriages there was always one who, on trips, did all the collecting— of maps, guides, theater programs, memorable newspapers, endless photographs, and the detritus of travel. In their marriage, Reed did the keeping. Since they had enough room, Kate confined her grumbling to outworn kitchen utensils and broken appliances. In a perfect society, appliances would be fixed and not tossed away to add to the ever-growing mountain of garbage and rejected non-biodegradable materials. Since no one in the United States could afford to fix appliances or to pay anyone else to, Kate saw little point in keeping them. She and Reed had, however, agreed without ever actually discussing it that he would hoard all his mementos without comments from her, and she would be permitted to discard any gadget that no longer worked. It made for an agreeable companionship.

Which was why Reed was able, after some burrowing, to produce a guide to Geneva written in French and acquired when, as a child after World War II, he had visited Geneva with his parents. Entitled *Les Guides Blues Illustrés: Genève et ses environs,* it had been published in 1937; the Swiss, having presumably remained unchanged by the war, had not required a new guide because it had ended. In Switzerland, Reed remarked as he turned it over, nothing changes. Of course, he pointed out, where the guide refers to the "palais de la Société de Nations" one must assume that the League of Nations has departed, leaving some other international organization hopefully in its wake to occupy its building. All else could be counted on to have altered little if at all. That, he concluded, is the whole point about Switzerland.

"Have they given women the vote yet?" Kate asked.

"Probably, although there may be a canton here or there that has held out. I do hope you are not going to Switzerland to start a revolution; there are better places for that."

"I'm going to talk to a woman who believes in burning the private letters of those connected to famous writers. I only hope that she will talk to me, not least because, in the deepest, least scholarly part of my being, I agree with her. Except for the fact that Gabrielle is dead and beyond having her privacy invaded, while we struggle on in a dreary world that she, in her privacy, may have been able to illuminate and may illuminate yet."

"Remember that bit for the woman in Geneva," Reed said; "it's very good."

Kate buried her nose in the guide, snubbing him.

She too had been to Geneva in her youth, but remembered little except the lake, the bridge across it, and the island named after Rousseau and boasting a statue of him. There was also, she seemed to remember, a monument to the Reformation with a statue of Calvin, to whom she had taken an instant and intense dislike. Rousseau she had in extreme youth rather admired; it was only when she encountered the destiny he had planned for Sophie while outlining the education of Emile that she had withdrawn that admiration.

Kate was, in truth, a poor traveler, going to places willingly enough if there was reason, but growing rapidly bored with sightseeing, an undertaking her mother had carried out with all the vigor of one desperate to acquire what she had been told was significant but without the usual concomitance of significance: risk. Sometime, Kate thought, there will be something my mother admired that I shall also learn to admire, but I cannot imagine what it will be.

Geneva was not the dearer for reminding Kate of her mother; little was. She therefore got down to business: after settling herself into her admirable Swiss hotel room and flushing the very Swiss and because wholly silent, strangely disconcerting toilet, she telephoned Nellie at her office. Nellie was pleasant, if formal, and invited Kate to a restaurant, name, address, and directions given, for dinner. Kate accepted and sat down to pull together her thoughts. When one had so many questions, it was well to order them.

As it turned out, however, once they had been seated in

a family sort of restaurant where Nellie apparently felt comfortable, had ordered, and Kate had been served with a larger portion than she could reasonably eat in a week, Nellie seemed more inclined to ask questions than to answer them. Like Dorinda and, of course, Anne, Nellie was over sixty, but Kate could not easily escape the conviction that she was the youngest of them all. Having inherited her grandmother's English coloring and skin, Nellie looked as though she could be any age at all, one age one minute, another the next. Dorinda, on the other hand, despite her unchanging features, had given the impression of welcoming the evidence of her years and the relief she found in no longer being young.

If Nellie was, to Kate's relief, willing to talk, it soon became clear that Gabrielle was not the main topic of her conversation.

"I've spoken to Dorinda about you," Nellie said. "I called her the other day. She seemed astonished to hear from me on the telephone and assumed a catastrophe. She and I are the generation who still think long-distance calls spell emergency. But I, of course, am used to it now, from my work. I asked her about you, in fact. I wanted to know more about you; for my own reasons. I hope you won't feel I've got you here on false pretensions."

"Not if we can also talk about Gabrielle," Kate said. "Later if you like."

"Of course. Dorinda said you were a detective, a private eye."

"Wholly inaccurate," Kate said with more emphasis than seemed warranted. "Sorry to be so downright about it, but I'm not really a detective and certainly not a private investigator. For one thing, they get paid."

"I am willing to pay," Nellie said, to Kate's horror. Was not she, after all, the one who was supposed to be asking the questions, the one who had crossed the ocean in considerable discomfort as was the condition of air travel these days, the one forced to the recontemplation of Rousseau and Calvin and silently flushing toilets? "Nellie," Kate said, calling on all her patience. "I don't want money, I don't take money, except as a salary from a university for the performance of clearly defined academic duties. I had hoped," she added as a way of bringing the conversation around to Gabrielle, "to make some money, a modest amount, from a biography of your grandmother, but otherwise I am totally and forever an amateur."

"But you have solved crimes; even murder, no?"

Kate noticed that Nellie, perfect in so many languages, occasionally permitted herself a foreign intonation. "Not exactly," Kate said. "That is, yes, but with reservations."

"Reservations?" Nellie was clearly puzzled.

"A joke," Kate said. "Woody Allen's. His response when he was asked if he was Jewish."

"I see," said Nellie, who clearly didn't. "You detect when the spirit moves you."

"More or less. But why don't we talk about you; you can hardly have expected me to fly all the way from New York to Geneva to talk about myself."

"I'll offer a trade," Nellie said.

"A trade?" Kate had reached, she realized, the moment in certain conversations when she found herself merely echoing the words of her interlocutor. It was evidence of unhappiness.

"Let us just chatter," Nellie said. "I'm being a poor hostess, harrying you. Have you ever been to Geneva before?''

"Once," Kate said. "Perhaps after dinner we can go and look at the lake with Rousseau in the middle; I remember that. Is it safe at this time to walk there?"

"Switzerland is nowhere as safe as it was," Nellie said, "but it is still safer than most places."

"How long have you been working in Geneva?" Kate asked, and by mutual agreement they talked of current events and current occupations.

When Nellie had paid the bill, and they had left, wandering, Kate assumed, toward the Rousseau lake, Nellie began to talk earnestly, as though walking loosened her inhibitions. "You must wonder what I could possibly want to trade, or have to trade for that matter," she began.

"Rather," Kate said.

"I'm sorry about the letters, about having burned them. That is, to be honest, I'm sorry for you, but I still feel certain I did the right thing. Grandma was a very private person; she would have hated her letters being read years later by total strangers whose only interest was in Poppop. You have to believe me, she really would have minded."

"I believe you. That is hardly the question. People who burn letters are in some ways less difficult to understand than those who preserve them. I know a poet whose poetry I don't happen to admire who saves carbons of all his letters, convinced someone will want to do a biography of him; the fact is, that very impulse to save copies of his letters is identical with his failure as a poet."

"Grandma was not a poet, and she did not keep carbons."

"You must forgive me if I tend to wander off in all

directions," Kate said. "My point was that letters may be inversely important to the tendency to burn them."

"Yes," Nellie said, "I understand that. You are a very perceptive person."

Kate resisted her usual inclination to deny compliments. "My point really is that your grandmother was probably, almost certainly, a more interesting person than anyone had thought; I sometimes suspect more interesting, even, than her famous husband. Since women in the past have a dreadful tendency to disappear into a cloud of anonymity and silence, one does feel impelled in some cases, like this one, to recover their voices and their stories."

"But, at times their stories are other people's stories too—ones they may not have any right to tell, no?"

"Why? Should not everyone have a right?" Kate asked. "Emmanuel Foxx told his story, and what he thought of as hers into the bargain. It's time we heard her story, don't you agree?"

"I wasn't thinking of Poppop," Nellie said. "I don't care what story they tell about him. I was thinking of Emile."

"Emile?" Kate asked, staring out at the statue of Rousseau, or rather where she knew it to be on the island, wondering what his famous book had to do with all this. And then she remembered. "Emile. The son. Your father," she heard herself saying like an actor in a badly written play. "I'm sorry," she added. "I seemed to have forgotten for a moment."

"Everyone forgot him," Nellie said. "That's the whole point; don't you see?"

"Well," Kate said, "not exactly." It *was* amazing,

really, how little Emile figured in all the biographical accounts, despite Foxx's joy at his birth. Even Anne seemed to have had to be reminded, when buying her nightwear, who he was. There is surely nothing worse than being the son of a famous father.

"I'll walk you back to your hotel," Nellie said, turning all the way around and setting off with Kate in the opposite direction. "You must be tired; jet lag and all that; they say your body gets out of its natural rhythms. Shall we talk tomorrow?"

"I have little else to do here," Kate said. "Nothing, really. I'll be happy to talk for as long as you like. I take it you really have burned the letters?"

"Yes," Nellie said; "I burned them. All of them I could find."

Kate wanted to ask her if she had read Anne's memoir; if Gabrielle had talked to Nellie about those papers. If Nellie was interested in the money that might be earned through them. All those questions had better wait for tomorrow.

"Do you work all day?" Kate asked.

"I shall take the afternoon off. We shall go sightseeing and talk. It is easier to talk when sightseeing, is it not?"

Not, Kate would have liked to say; definitely not. But the asker of questions, whether professional or amateur or, as in this case, an awkward combination of both, must let the answerer choose the ambience. Unless of course one were le Carré's Smiley and could have people swept up off pavements and delivered to secret houses where they were questioned and confined and even beaten up if they didn't properly respond. No wonder all the interesting people joined the secret service, Kate thought. In books, anyway.

She had an idea though that Smiley was the exception, and that most people in the secret service of any country were no nearer to the truth than the rest of us.

Kate had great difficulty falling asleep: strange bed, strange country, strange situation. Smiley never got much sleep either. Hush, hush, she said to herself, whisper who dares. Le Carré, of course, knew Christopher Robin's England was as dead as Kate's WASP America, and a good thing too. But who is there who does not occasionally recall, even with irony, those simpler times? With the secret service, she thought, it is Russia and the United States; with me it is men and women, and who knows which shall first achieve reconciliation?

At which point, happily, she slept.

Nellie and Kate began their afternoon lunching at an outdoor café watching the passing scene. At least, they were supposed to be watching it, but by the end of the lunch Kate could not have told you if a herd of elephants had passed. As it happened, Kate's gaze was fixed on Nellie as though she expected her to undergo some fundamental transformation which, in a sense, she was in the process of doing.

"Emile didn't die during the war," Nellie said.

Kate stared at her. This woman is over sixty, she had to keep reminding herself. Somehow, after reading Anne's memoir, the three of them remained young to her. Staring at Nellie, who was certainly not an adolescent, in no way shook that conviction. Perhaps, Kate thought, it is because Dorinda seems to me, and in a way Nellie too, as though they were not winding down their lives but starting them over; well, not over, exactly, but going off on a new tack. Dorinda had as much as said so. And yet, Kate thought, doing some fast arithmetic in her head, Emile must be eighty-three if he's a day, supposing he is living. A large suppose.

"Has anyone seen him lately?" Kate asked.

"Not lately," Nellie said. "Emile died a few years ago. But I saw him more than ten years after he disappeared. When I went to London to see Gabrielle, after Dorinda's wedding."

"Did you know he was alive before you heard from him?"

"None of us knew anything for sure. He had gone off to join the Resistance, about the time I left for America. That was what we all assumed or were led to assume. Gabrielle had a letter or two from him just after he left—yes, I burned those too—and in 1942 Poppop died. Then, sometime in 1944 Gabrielle heard from a man who said he had been in the Resistance with Emile; he said that Emile had died in a raid on a farm where he was hiding. The letter writer added that he had a few of Emile's belongings, and would return them to Gabrielle or, if he did not survive, see that they were returned after the war. He did survive and after the war Gabrielle received a package with Emile's watch in it, and a picture of me as a baby he used to carry with him, and a few other things. I imagine Emile got rid of everything that reminded him of who he was and the life he had lived."

Kate pondered this. "Is there any evidence that Emile didn't send the package himself?" she asked.

"I suspect he really got someone to send it for him, the same person who wrote the first letter. What is infinitely puzzling to me was why he wanted to see me. I could understand his wanting to see Gabrielle—she had adored him—but why me?"

"You look like Gabrielle," Kate said. "At least, like the pictures I've seen of her; perhaps you were able to be you and remind him of her. A romantic thought."

"Very romantic," Nellie said, turning a stemmed glass between her fingers. "And like most romantic thoughts, powerfully convincing. You'd never guess how many people have seen that resemblance, have told me I am Gabrielle again, reborn to Emile. Even I used to pride myself on how much I looked like her. What people overlooked, however, was that Emmanuel Foxx was English too."

Kate stared at Nellie, her brain refusing for a moment to comprehend what she thought was being told to her. A long silence hung between them.

Nellie broke it.

"I am no relation whatever to Gabrielle," she said; "no relation by blood or biology, that is. I'm very much of a relation if love is the criterion."

"It seems to have been an extremely well-kept secret," Kate said at last for something to say.

"Gabrielle knew, of course. Hilda would have done anything to bear a child to a genius. Oh, I suspect she seduced Emile shortly afterward, to cover her tracks. To do her justice, if there is any justice to be done, she probably would have kept the secret from Emile, from everyone, even, after a time, herself. But Poppop couldn't keep from gloating; he couldn't keep his smirking pride at having a daughter off his face. Oh, he tried to remember, I've no doubt, to call me his granddaughter, but Poppop never saw any reason to hide his light under a bushel. Emmanuel had always wanted another child, but it had never happened; I don't know why. Perhaps Gabrielle made sure it never happened. Emmanuel was famous for hating contraception, but she may not have told him; I doubt she told him anything she didn't want to."

"How long have you known?"

"Probably always. But denial or repression or whatever you choose to call it is a comfortable way of life. I never knew in the sense of having to know until Emile told me in 1951, just after Dorinda's wedding. He felt he'd been cheated all his life, and I suspect he had been. But what he couldn't stand was being constantly reminded of how great, how interesting, how famous his father was. So with the opportunity provided by the war, when so many records were lost or confused, to say nothing of people and whole countries if it comes to that, he simply decided to die and begin another life."

"Why did he want to tell you?"

"Ah, there you are. That's the question, isn't it? He needed to have someone know. Anyway, Gabrielle knew, he was sure of that. He told me to make sure no one else would ever find out. He didn't know if it was in any of the letters, but he wanted everything I could get my hands on burned. I'm sure Gabrielle never wrote of it, or mentioned it at all—I realize now that's why she detested Hilda—but Emile was intent on covering all the tracks. I could understand why. Can't you?"

Kate was not certain this was really a question, or how to answer it if it were. But apparently Nellie wanted an answer, and waited for one, still twirling her glass.

"Yet Gabrielle loved you very much," Kate finally said.

"I know. I think back at how I must have hurt her, wanting so badly to go to America. But life was awful at home. If I had been older, and without the overwhelming selfishness of adolescence, I would have stayed to make Gabrielle's life a

141

little easier. She must have guessed how ill Poppop really was; she always knew everything, Gabrielle did. But I couldn't wait to get away, dearly as I loved her. Don't you see, that's why now I have to do what she would have wanted me to do. I know in my heart that Gabrielle would have protected Emile, would not have wanted this to come out and hurt him more than he had already been hurt.''

For the first time since they had ordered their lunch, Kate focused her eyes on distant things, the street, the people, the cars. On the opposite sidewalk a woman and child walked along as they might have walked anywhere in the Western world. Gabrielle must have walked with Emile just so, and later, with Nellie. Now, Nellie was waiting for her to speak when she could think of nothing to say or, to be more exact, nothing suitable to say.

When Reed hears of this, Kate thought, he will be fascinated to know what sort of revelation it took to render me speechless. Kate could have responded to an immediate loss, or to a present problem however intricate and insoluble. But this story from the past, so filled with pain for those no longer here to feel it (and Kate had no doubt Emile felt it to the end), left Kate speechless.

"Did you ever try to see Emile again?" she finally asked.

"No," Nellie said. "He married a simple French woman, a peasant really, and they lived in the French countryside, a peaceful life, after all. I don't think anyone around them had even heard of Emmanuel Foxx. Of course, the elegant people were encroaching, but not too near. Emile had told me he pretended to know no English, and to find their French difficult.''

"So he played a game to the end."

"Not a special game. Emile and I after him thought of

languages as a game; we spoke so many. Poppop used to say he didn't want to hear English around him, he wanted to preserve it for his writing; he wanted only the English speech of his characters in his ears. So at home they always spoke something else, and did when I came along. Gabrielle spoke English to me, but only when Poppop was not around; it was our private language."

"Is it strange that she loved you, or only my stupid conventional mind that thinks so?"

"I asked myself that," Nellie said. "She was the perfect figure of love for me. Oh, I found Poppop and even Emile when he was around—I called him Pa—fun and somehow more exciting than Gabrielle. We are all geared to respond to men who appear seldom and smelling delightfully of adventure. But she was the one I loved. When I went to America and got to know Anne, I pitied her because she had no loving mother in her life. Her own mother was stern, not warm at all, always warning of dangers, and Eleanor was reserved, and saved her rather frantic love for Dorinda, though she was kind to all of us. But I had had this great woman to love me. Somehow, when I learned she wasn't my grandmother, it no longer mattered to me. Whether it ever mattered to her, I don't know; I don't think so. But I don't pretend to understand it."

"Did you see much of your real mother, Hilda?" Kate asked, choosing it as the least important, least emotional question she could think of. They needed time to get back to the heart of the conversation.

"Not a great deal. She fussed over me when I was a baby, but somehow I always knew she wished I had been a boy. Poppop made a big fuss about wanting me to be the same sex as his heroine, and I guess she played with me and

143

that fantasy for a time. But there were nurses. It was from them Gabrielle rescued me. I can't bear, you see, to have her analyzed, and glared at, and smirked about by people who haven't a clue, really, of what a gem she was, what a sweet, sweet woman. Not gooey, the way that sounds, forceful really, but oh so warm."

"I have to ask you, Nellie. Do you know about Anne's memoir?"

"Oh, yes. She sent me a copy. With a letter explaining about the papers, about how if she sold them, and she might have to, she would let me know because I would get half the money. She also said she felt she ought to offer me all the money, but she badly needed it. She lives in New York now, and it's terribly expensive there, even though she has a good job. And the man she lives with can't work. He's had a breakdown or something.

"I'm afraid I gave you the impression that Dorinda and Anne and I aren't really in touch when I said what I did about long-distance telephone calls. The fact is we stay wonderfully in touch now, all three of us, with letters, and occasional calls, and more occasional visits. I think Dorinda was startled by my call because she feared something had gone wrong. But we are in touch, all three of us, we really are. I'm sorry; I'm afraid I've got to the chattering stage."

She put down her glass, and Kate took her hand. "Were you afraid," Kate asked, "that I would do Gabrielle some damage; reveal Emile's secret? Is that what worries you?"

"When I say we were in touch," Nellie went on, as though she hadn't heard even though she was answering Kate's question, "I meant that we had all three talked about you, about your doing the biography. We had to decide what to do. I don't want the story of Gabrielle's life, or

Emile's either, to come out. They were sad lives, and I don't think there's much point in writing about them. I mean, I don't think you'll be missing out on much by not doing the biography.''

Not much, Kate thought, just the whole basis on which I've planned my life for the next five years or so. Well, did that really matter? Damn it, Gabrielle mattered. She remained this enigma in the center of this great phenomenon of high modernism. Surely she had a right to be heard. And how did Nellie know she might not have wanted her story to be told? Certainly she had gone to enough trouble to save those papers, whatever they were.

Nellie had waited for Kate to digest her comment; she knew its implications.

"Wouldn't it be possible," Kate asked, "to write a life of Gabrielle and leave Emile out; let him disappear in 1944, simply leave the story as we have all believed it up to now?"

"It would be possible," Nellie said, "but do you think you could do that?"

Kate pondered it. "No," she said. "You're right, I couldn't. I couldn't know something and not say it. Not these days. That's how biographies used to be written in the bad old times, but not anymore. Honesty and facing facts may not be worth much, but today it's just about all we've got. I think I'd rather abandon the whole project."

"There's something you haven't thought of, not having had the time."

"There's a lot I haven't thought of," Kate said. "A thousand things. But do any of them make any difference?"

"What you haven't thought of," Nellie persisted as though Kate had not spoken, "is how we have trusted you."

"Have you? You're right, I hadn't noticed."

"Kate, I'm afraid you're in shock. Think a minute. I've told you the truth. I've offered a trade. But what's to stop you from printing what I've told you and telling me, 'Sorry, you were wrong to trust me,' as so many journalists do?"

"I'm not a journalist."

"You're a detective, whatever you want to call yourself. You might have found out anyway. This way, we can make a trade."

"Let's walk," Kate said, not yet ready to confront what she suspected was coming. "I've got to get the blood moving around again."

They set out again for the lake without discussing it. Kate felt like someone who had learned the lines for one play and found herself in another for which, mysteriously, she was supposed to know her part. She realized that above all she needed time to digest what she had heard, to think it through.

"Of course," Nellie said. "But you must just let me tell you our side of the trade. Since I am absolutely certain that Gabrielle would not have wanted anyone to discover or tell the truth or even a version of the truth about her life, I can be pretty certain, and Anne agrees, that the papers Gabrielle was so eager to save must not be autobiographical—at least, they probably don't tell the truth about Emile and me and Poppop. But they are probably of great interest. What I thought, and Anne has agreed, is that we could let you see them, and then, if you thought them interesting, you could edit them for publication in place of the biography. You don't have to answer; just think about it. I'll call you tomorrow."

Kate nodded and turned toward her hotel. She sensed

rather than saw Nellie stand and watched her go. As though unable to consider the larger aspects of this situation, she started imagining herself telling Simon Pearlstine that she was abandoning the biography to bring out an edition of Gabrielle's writing. He would demand the advance back; well, she would give it back. And then?

When Kate reached her hotel she found a message from Simon asking how she was getting on; would she call and tell him? Kate was beyond figuring out what time it was now in New York. She found the hotel's fax machine and, for the first time in her life, sent one. It said: "Having wonderful time; wish you were here." Not, she thought, having finally reached her room and collapsed on the bed, too far from the truth. Reed would be preferable, but even Simon would be someone to talk to. Except, of course, that she must not tell anyone but Reed what she had heard. Whatever the bargain, or trade as Nellie called it, whatever Kate's decision, she understood she was not free to consult anyone else. What had begun as a biography was, before her eyes, transforming itself into something else, as yet vague and troubling. Her literary self had become a detective, not, as always before, the other way around.

Seven

KATE flew back to New York with her thoughts chasing each other through her head; their resolving themselves into an idea was less probable than their leaving her confused, sleepless, and haunted by demons. If she dozed for a moment, characters from the Foxx drama came to derange her with their preposterous acts and suggestions. Several of the airplane's martinis in small bottles failed either to encourage sleep or to discourage the ghosts. But at least by the time she had landed, hungry (for who can eat airline food?) and exhausted, she had made up her mind to arrange a meeting with Anne Gringold as soon as possible.

One thing was sufficiently clear: Dorinda and Nellie, while not exactly lying to her, had doled out the truth with great care, allowing it slowly to contradict previous impressions. With Anne, the situation might be different, for Kate had read Anne's memoir, and so would begin with a wider base on which to build her theories. And certainly it was theories, however imprecise, that she required. Such as, why would the secret about who Nellie's father was, after the death of all the principals, be so appalling? These days, such revelations were hardly even startling, at least after the first all-over sense of wonder. Nellie would become of more interest to the world, which was hardly a fate avoided by most people. Emile and Gabrielle were dead and beyond injury. Emmanuel Foxx's reputation might be strengthened in some quarters and reduced in others, but it would probably not make any fundamental difference to anyone's opinion of his major novel or any of his other works.

But to those for whom discretion and secrecy were a way of life, the public rendition of one's family scandals was to be avoided at any cost. And why shouldn't Nellie have grown sick to death of being cultivated as Foxx's granddaughter, let alone wish to be further bombarded by those who would now know that her relation to the great man was one generation closer?

Obviously, Anne was the next step for Kate, less in the hope of learning the story of Anne's life or Anne's secrets, if any, which were, after all, peripheral, than the substance and subject of the papers Gabrielle had left with her. After this observation (upon which Kate would soon look back with as much sense of irony and bemused good humor as she could muster) she went to sleep for ten hours and awakened to a large breakfast, a conversation with Reed in which she told him nothing and told him she had told him nothing being not yet ready to tell anyone anything.

Eventually, she reached Anne on the telephone. Yes, Anne would see her, two days hence, wherever she, Kate, liked. Kate suggested her own apartment, and Anne agreed.

It occurred to Kate that she had seen none of this trio in her own domicile. Only Eleanor had received Kate in her home. For all Kate really knew, the other three might live in spaceships circling the globe. Anything, Kate was beginning to think, was possible with those three.

When Anne arrived for their interview, Kate's first impression was what a diffuse lot, as far as looks went, the trio was. Anne had clearly run to fat, an unkind way to put it, Kate admonished herself. She was solid and evidently indifferent, in these days of devotion to the presentation of one's face and body, to her appearance. Her demeanor was more open than that of either Dorinda or Nellie, but then it was, after all, Anne who had written the memoir, Anne about whom most was already known, Anne who had been, through her memoir, the first to speak to Kate.

Kate offered her a drink and to Kate's pleasure she accepted a beer. Kate joined her in one, and when they had settled down with their glasses, Anne remarked on how pleasant it was to sit in this comfortable room on an ordinary afternoon and drink beer. "I feel quite a truant," she said. "Perhaps I shall now find the courage to take off an afternoon and go to a ball game. Except that there aren't many baseball games played on weekday afternoons anymore, are there?"

"Perhaps we can go together," Kate said. "I haven't been to a baseball game in donkey's years, whatever they are; a long time anyway." We are beginning very far from the subject, Kate thought, and yet we are not insincere. I would like to go to a ball game with Anne. "The Mets, of course," Kate added. "All my brothers are or were Yankee fans, so there's no question about that. My brothers and I share no opinions whatever, which is rather a comfort; one never has to consider giving them the benefit of the doubt."

"It's nice of you to begin with a personal revelation," Anne said, "since so many will obviously be expected of me. Not that I mind," she hastily added. "I can't imagine what it would be like to have brothers. Neither Nellie nor I has children, as I guess you know, and Dorinda has four sons, which is really going it a bit, Nellie and I feel."

"I saw Nellie in Geneva just a few days ago," Kate said. "But we never talked of her present life at all, just of the past. I had so many questions about the past I didn't feel it right to ask about the present; anyway, I loathe people who keep asking questions."

"Nellie has been married for years to a man who writes books on philosophy and theories of art, all in French, and all profound, and all close to incomprehensible, even, I understand, if you read French. They seem very happy. He can work anywhere, which is fortunate since Nellie tends to get moved around from time to time. Good beer." Anne sat back in her comfortable chair, clearly relishing the leisure, the pleasure of not being at work in an afternoon.

"Do you still work for a publishing firm?" Kate asked. "Of course your memoir ended thirty or so years ago, so perhaps that's a silly question?"

"Still the same job," Anne said. "More responsibility, more pay, still the same job. It's actually rather interesting, if you don't pretend you're selling anything more than a product. Not something sacred like books, I mean, just a product. You study the markets, develop selling and distributing techniques, use the computer inventively, and wish to God that the people who are supposed to fill orders, the warehouses and the accounting departments, did not make so many knuckle-headed mistakes. I'm very good at what I do, and the fact that it's not madly glamorous or innovative means I can go on doing it even now when I'm getting a bit long in the tooth. I root for the Mets too, though I wish to hell they hadn't gone in for ball girls. If a woman ever makes it into baseball, it should be because she plays so well they can't not hire her. Till then, I'd rather not have girlish legs in ridiculous uniforms cavorting around like playboy bunnies. You mustn't pay too much attention to me; I don't often get the chance to shoot my mouth off; I'm either too busy or too tired. What did you want to talk to me about? Surely not the Mets."

"As you probably know," Kate said, "I'm a literary type. As such, I couldn't help noticing that you ended your marvelous memoir the way Jane Austen ended her novels, rather too rapidly, as though you'd passed the interesting part and had to tie it all up as fast as possible, not much liking the way you had to end it."

"How tactfully you put it, and quite right too. The end was about Gabrielle's papers, but the story was really about me, as most stories are. I guess I knew readers, if any, would be rushing toward the inevitable end. No need to linger over it."

"It's an amazing story, the three of you there together, and you and Dorinda before that. It's a heartwarming story. I was rather relieved," Kate added, watching for Anne's reactions with some trepidation, "to find that Dorinda was such a nice person. One gathered from what you wrote and from her mother that she went through a long period of being, well, rather a prig, which was so different from her as a child and young woman."

"Yes. Dorinda's come round nicely. We all have. Might I say that we all realized that someone would decide one day to do a biography of Gabrielle, it was really inevitable, wasn't it, and when we heard it was you we were very pleased. I mean, it might have been someone less scholarly and less, well, intelligent, less able to understand what life was like when we were all young and modernism was at its height.''

"Am I to infer from that complimentary speech that you sent the memoir to Simon Pearlstine *after* deciding that I should do the biography—perhaps to add weight to that inducement?"

"Nellie and Dorinda both said you were clever as well as intelligent—a detective as well as a literary type. I see they were right."

"Simon Pearlstine certainly went a considerable way toward giving me a somewhat different impression. But no doubt he was covering his ass, as they say in the big crude world. You said you wanted it especially for my eyes."

"Yours only. It was to encourage you, specifically you, to do the biography of Gabrielle. Dorinda only sent it to Pearlstine after she was able to learn from that wonderful grapevine she still has her ear to that there was a real chance he was going to pursue you. There are no secrets in publishing, and my own sources confirmed Dorinda's. You might wonder why I didn't just send it to you myself. Partly, Dorinda is the one among us who does that sort of thing; but the truth is, I wanted this to reach Pearlstine indirectly, as a faintly mysterious document. Also, I had not quite overcome the need for distance I felt so acutely after I took Gabrielle's papers to the bank in London. Anyway, we had looked into you and your doings, taking rather a long time and special care about it, well, mostly

Dorinda did, but she had some help from me, and we definitely determined that you were exactly the right person. So when Pearlstine approached you, we went, so to speak, into action. You were chosen.'' Anne smiled.

"You seem to mean," Kate said with sufficient asperity to indicate that she was not being carried away by compliments, "if I understood Nellie and she was certainly clear, you sent it to encourage me *not* to do the biography of Gabrielle."

Anne smiled and put down her empty glass. "Well, not a usual biography; but an elegant portrait of Gabrielle as an introduction to your edition of her writings."

"Which you spirited off at her insistence?"

"Exactly. Our feeling is that the lives of marginal people like the three of us and Emile are not what's really important. What's important, because it's where all her real life went, was what Gabrielle wrote."

"Another beer?"

"In a minute," Anne said.

"You imply she was writing much of her life. Why did none of it ever appear, why did no one know of it or mention it until that moment when she gave you the papers in Kensington, practically Knightsbridge?"

"You can't imagine even for a moment that Emmanuel Foxx the great creator could have borne her writing anything at any time. *He* was the writer, she was his muse, at least at best; his minion, really, not to say his servant. She kept all her writing secret, all tucked away. I don't know when she began writing; no one does. It's possible that she wrote the greater part of it all after Foxx's death, when she was alone in Paris. Perhaps it was when she had finished writing that she decided to move back to England. Or perhaps she wanted to finish up in England; honestly, one doesn't know.''

"Wouldn't the actual papers themselves tell you something? The age of the paper, the ink, the watermarks, that sort of thing? Did you notice anything?"

"Not me," Anne said. "Do let's have another beer; it's so pleasant, drinking and talking like this. At that time in London I felt as though I had some sort of divine command to follow; I shuffled those papers into a bank so fast, I never really got a look at them at all." Anne pushed herself up from the deep chair where she had happily been lolling and followed Kate into the kitchen. "My thought," she said to Kate's back as Kate opened the beers, "is that you and I would look at them when we remove them from the bank."

"Where is the bank?" Kate asked when they were once more happily ensconced. They could hear the telephone ringing in the distance. "Wonderful things, answering machines," Kate said. "I fought them as I have fought every new dehumanizing device that has come along, but in the end one succumbs and has to admit to the benefits. I have arranged whole events without ever speaking directly to the other person involved. Is it progress or disaster, or are these just another name for convenience?"

"The bank is in England," Anne said, grinning at Kate to show she agreed about the telephone machine, but would honorably avoid any temptations to defer discussing the important subject before them. "In London. The nearest one at the time. I've gone on paying all these years for the vault, which has been a bit of a burden, but Eleanor, bless her, agreed to contribute once I'd told her the story of the papers. She even gave me a retroactive sum, so to speak. Eleanor is great. Really great.''

"I liked her very much," Kate said. "Am I being invited to accompany you to London for the first real look at Gabrielle's leavings?"

"You are. I thought of asking Eleanor, but she's a bit old for traipsing around, strongly as I consider it her right. Sig's money of course, but it was Eleanor who had the instincts about Gabrielle and Nellie. Eleanor always had the right instincts, except in choosing a husband. But even there, she wouldn't have been able to help the Foxxes if she hadn't married Sig.''

Kate had by now caught on to the fact that Anne may have appeared to ramble in her conversation, but her topics and observations, as well as her emphases, were as carefully orchestrated as any musical score. Kate put down her glass and leaned forward to address Anne with body language as well as words.

"Look here, Anne, I've been handled by the three of you—you and Dorinda and Nellie, I mean—with all the delicacy of some spy operation. I don't want to say I feel set up, that would be a bit crude and not accurate, but I do have the sense of being about to receive a proposition that is going to be startling and very carefully thought out. Do you think I might have it? That is, of course, if you and Dorinda and Nellie have decided you're the ones to inform me and today's the day I'm to be informed?"

"You're hard to set up," Anne said, laughing. "You were supposed to ask me about Sig; that was your next line: a question about Eleanor and Sig. I like to take things in order."

"That," Kate said, "is fairly obvious. All right, consider yourself asked the appropriate question about Eleanor and Sig. Like why should you care what their relationship was, apart from what you've written in your memoir?"

"I showed the memoir to Eleanor, or rather, I read it to her. She was only ninety then, or nearly, but she preferred to listen. Eleanor always was a good listener; I guess listening was the major part of what she did, apart from arranging to make everyone's life easier." Anne sipped her beer. "Eleanor liked my memoir. I apologized for what I had said about the Goddards' generosity; it sounded a little mean-spirited when I read it out that way, but Eleanor wouldn't hear a word of it. 'You got it just right, Anne,' she told me, 'and so did Gabrielle. You all sensed the truth even if you didn't know it. Did you never guess?' Eleanor asked me. 'Guess what?' I naturally said."

"Another mistaken father?" Kate asked.

"Clever! You *are* clever," Anne said. "Though of course I didn't have the example of Nellie's parentage to give me a hint, as you did. Anyway, I didn't guess at all, and poor Eleanor wondered if she ought to have mentioned it. In the end she told me. I think she always meant to; I think one of the things she had decided on when she grew old was honesty, getting through the lies we live, and tell ourselves, and tell each other. Well, you've had no trouble with it."

"I wasn't really involved," Kate said. "It's easy to guess things you haven't an emotional stake in."

"Sig was my father. That was why they were so willing to take me in, even if my mother did have her doubts. But at least it wasn't charity. The one thing I never understood about my mother was why she was willing to take charity;

she was so proud, and so insistent on holding up her end, holding up her head she used to say. But if he was my father, he owed me. Only me, never her. She never took a thing from him, never gave him the time of day again, although they met from time to time."

"He didn't dance with her at Dorinda's wedding?" Kate asked. "That was someone else?"

"Definitely someone else, though I think she danced there as a kind of abandon, a moment when the pretense didn't need to be maintained. After all, she had been invited as my mother, because I was so much a part of the Goddard family; nothing could change that. That's an odd thing for you to ask, really."

"Her dancing impressed me," Kate said. "Does Dorinda know?"

"Dorinda and Nellie both know now. I think, I really do think, we all three know everything worth telling."

"Sig was dead by the time you read your memoir to Eleanor."

"Long dead. It's odd to think of; I still muse about it, in a humorous sort of way. Sig always wanted a son, and he got two daughters at almost the same moment. Hilda wanted a son, and she got a daughter too, at almost the same moment. We were all three close when we were young, and we're close again now. It's as though Dorinda had gone under a spell for a time, and we all went under it with her; I'm glad it's over. More than that," and Kate had the sense of Anne's saying something she had not quite formulated, not quite intended to say for a while yet, "we all have a second chance, a chance to live our friendship, to attend to what matters. And, most of all, a second chance for Gabrielle. Do you think all women really have a second chance, even if life hasn't given them a clear first chance?''

"The history of the English novel is like that," Kate said, sensing the need for an interval of impersonality. "From the very beginning, from *Tom Jones* and *Moll Flanders* up until Hardy, it was all about second chances. Jane Austen's *Persuasion* is a fine example. And then with Hardy, second chances lost their force. Think of *The Mayor of Casterbridge;* an obvious example, but there are many others. I have a feeling now that, for women at any rate, second chances may be coming back." Kate drank her beer and smiled at Anne.

"What did Dorinda say about Sig being your father as well as hers?" she asked.

"She said it shows you female genes are more powerful, at least for women, since we don't look any more alike than our mothers, whom we both resemble. Nellie actually looks more like Sig, but she's the daughter of his sister. Dorinda very nicely said we couldn't have been closer if we had known we were half-sisters, and that's quite simply true. And now it's even truer, since we know."

"Nellie seemed more obviously a relation," Kate said. "Yet you and Nellie were as closely related as the other two. It all seems to go to prove how little difference fathers make."

"Except to the fathers. What Nellie told you about herself made an enormous difference to Emile, I assure you. And if Eleanor had been anyone other than who she was, that fact of my father would have made an enormous difference to her."

"Was your mother really married?"

"Oh, yes. I think she despised him, although no one ever

159

spoke of him. In fact, when I asked her about him, she said he made no difference to me and I should not bother my head about him, which was closer to the truth than I ever guessed. He took off when my mother became pregnant; he didn't want responsibility. Not that he knew I wasn't his. I did ask Eleanor that. She said he never knew, and my mother wanted it that way. He died sometime later; that she did hear, but she never married again. I don't believe any one of her sisters knew the truth; I'm sure they didn't. They probably just thought my mother was being smart when she let the Goddards take me over.''

"Do you think Eleanor always knew?''

"Oh, yes. She was the one who helped my mother to get work, at which she was really very successful and highly paid. She only died a few years ago, you know, and she'd saved a good bit which came to me; I only wish she'd managed to spend it a little more wildly in her old age, but thrift with her was a passion. I realize now that when Dorinda suggested my coming to live with them, Eleanor seized on the idea, although she no doubt made it appear that Dorinda was once again getting her own way. I never changed a word of that memoir after I found out the truth. And yet, now you've read it, you know nothing in it contradicts that fact when you discover it. Yet nothing really required it either. I think it's a lesson in biography; perhaps facts don't matter all that much.''

"I'm afraid my position is asking impertinent questions,'' Kate said. "But you said your mother left you 'a good bit,' and Nellie said you were hard up. I know 'good bits' are of different sizes, but was Nellie telling the truth?''

"She exaggerated a little. Len—the one in the memoir— lives with me now. He married someone else, but it didn't finally last. He's only got his pension and social security, but we like to take expensive trips on our vacations, and he likes to come with me when I travel on business. I think Nellie was adding another incentive to urge you to publish the papers, the hope of increasing my income. And it will increase it if you do, in a most welcome way. Nellie could use the income too, not out of desperate need, but she isn't paid all that much and her husband makes very little from his books. We all do hope you'll want to publish the papers."

"Do you mind if I talk to Dorinda again before I decide whether to go with you to London or not?"

"Of course you must see Dorinda whenever you want. You don't really have to come to London; I could go and ship the papers back. But I'd rather you came."

"If I go on with this quite mad scheme, I'll come," Kate said. "After all, I have taken the whole year off, and what's that for if not popping around the world? Besides, the simple truth is that I'm dying to see those papers—consumed, you might even say—so of course I'll come."

Anne rose to leave. "It's been a lovely afternoon, lovely getting to know you, as the governess said in the song to the children of the king of Siam. The three of us saw that when we were young together." Anne started to giggle. "I just remembered what Dorinda said when I told her about Sig being my father. 'Aha,' she said; 'I should have known from a villainous trick of thine eye and a foolish hanging of thy nether lip.' We read *Henry IV, Part I* in school. Of course, I wondered, we both did, how he had seduced my mother, whom he must have come across working in his house or someone else's. But it doesn't take much imagination. He was a reprobate and a charming one; my mother

161

must have had some profound desires only partly buried. As I noticed when she danced. I never liked her, nor, I think, she me very much, but I did admire her, and I'm glad I saw her dance.''

Kate walked to the door with Anne, denying herself the many questions still to be asked. Their trust of her was, when you came to consider it, quite amazing. No doubt, having once determined on their and Gabrielle's second chance, and having decided on Kate as their instrument, there was no turning back. She would see Dorinda again, and perhaps, just for the pleasure of it and because the chance might not be hers for long, Eleanor. Then she would go to London with Anne. After that—well, her decision was at least a clear one. Either she would do what they wanted or nothing at all. There was no other way in which she would tell the stories she had heard from the three of them nor any story she might in future hear.

In choosing to trust her, they had chosen well, and that, not unnaturally, endeared them to Kate. That other secrets might emerge to be reluctantly revealed was certainly possible. But once you decide to trust someone, you must trust them. Unless you are unmistakenly betrayed, there is never any turning back.

Eight

DORINDA, like Anne, said she would come to Kate's apartment. Their conversation had reached a point where restaurants could not provide the perfect ambience; nor did Kate want to enter one of the houses of the trio: she preferred to keep her metaphoric vision of them circling in space, like the stars that were supposed to be Ariadne and her children. Dorinda sat in the same chair Anne had sat in, but declined a beer; as the afternoon wore on, she said, she would welcome a sherry.

"You have really come to know us all," Dorinda said, looking around her frankly. "Nice room. I gather from Anne that you are now up-to-date on all our murky secrets. We do seem to have gone in for a lot of irregular fathering, not that I can see what difference it makes, except that Anne is now half-Jewish like Nellie and me. I tell Anne that's where she gets her business sense, but she points out that

I'm being illogical in the first place, since with the same father I have no business sense, and racist in the second. She's right, of course. Her mother had wonderful business sense. Anne always used to win these arguments, but I always ended thinking I had a point and I do now. Without the Sig input, Anne would probably have ended up like her mother's sisters, without a brain in her head. The Goddard genes vary, they are hardly pervasive, but they add a certain *je ne sais quoi*. Still, none of us is very Goddardlike as you may have noticed."

"So Anne said you said."

"Did she? Well, she also said you might do the Gabrielle bit; will you? We all think you would be wonderful, and we have a sort of three-musketeerish pact to revive Gabrielle without reviving her as wife and mother: on her own, you might say."

"I'm thinking about it," Kate said. "My problem, frankly, is that I find myself in the center of some sort of spy plot. I mean, each of you seems to have a cover story, and when that is removed, there's another story underneath. Le Carré has his characters say that no one can resist today's methods for extracting the truth from spies once they're caught, but I am not in anyone's secret service. So how am I to know when I've got the truth?"

"Ask away. We've told you all, and will tell you any bits we've forgotten if you just mention them. Since I dare say I'm the biggest mystery of the lot—at least so the other two keep telling me—I thought I ought to fill in a few lacunae that may be causing you anxiety, consciously or unconsciously."

Kate, who was thinking not so much of lacunae as of gaping holes, nodded encouragingly.

164

"Okay. First of all, I frankly admit," Dorinda said, "that I have played many roles in my time, like Shakespeare's Jaques, except that mine haven't gone neatly along according to conventional ideas of age, to say nothing of the fact that I was never a schoolboy with shining face, but I'm sure you see what I mean. You know about my wild and woolly youth from Anne. One would have thought it would reveal to me that men are not the sole and only answer to women's needs, but it didn't, at least, not for a long time. Dear Aunt Hilda never learned that at all, of course, and when her mad and superficial world went to pieces, so did she. Went to pieces, I mean, and Daddy had to haul her home on the 'last plane out of disaster,' as Auden says, only it was a ship. Unlike Hilda, I didn't go in for a famous man, I went in for a steady, dull one, equally wrong-headed but at least leaving me some years in which to be cocoonish and develop from a slug to a butterfly. Not that I'm really a butterfly, but compared to what I've been, the description is not wholly unwarranted. Do you want to hear about Mark Hansford?"

"Certainly," Kate said, feeling as though she were "it" in a game of blind man's bluff.

"He turned up at what might be called the moment of my awakening or the beginning of my transformation. He cured me of my past. He wanted my photographs for his book, and he immediately grasped that the way to get them was to diddle me as men do. And he succeeded; I let myself be diddled. Not only that, I found myself mouthing all the truisms of what I call my Arthur period: Anne is too feminist, there is a natural and unnatural way to love, you name it, I mouthed it, as long as it was conventional and not inclined to induce thought. I read a good quote recently, from someone named Wilson Mizener: 'I respect faith, but

165

doubt is what gets you an education.' Truest words ever spoken. Not that what I had could be called faith exactly; armor would be a better description. Anyway, it was when I saw myself going through this idiotic routine with Mark Hansford, and after he'd got the photographs and decided to try again with his wife, like something in a soap opera, I woke up like Rip Van Winkle to find everything changed, but in my case wonderfully so. And I don't really mind about the pictures, though I think you should use the one of Gabrielle at the window. I have the rights to it, so that will be okay."

"Your mother mentioned that Arthur was a bit, well, dull."

"Arthur was and is dull, and more than a bit. We're separating, actually. He's found a compliant nurse. I dare say he's been finding them for years, but this one wants marriage, which is bright of her. I'm trying to play the bereft and aging wife, partly for fun and partly on the advice of my lawyer, but it's uphill work I can assure you. It's money I'm after, all those years of being a proper wife to Arthur."

"Will you get it?"

"Oh, yes. Arthur really wants his nurse in holy matrimony, and the one who wants the divorce is the one who pays. I have him, therefore, by the short and curlies, a lovely sensation."

"You might want to marry again."

"I might, but don't hold your breath. All three of us, you see, ended up being nice to men, and I think I've done my share. Nellie and Anne are attached to their guys, who are at least intelligent and caring. I might have that sherry now."

As Anne had done, Dorinda came with Kate as she fetched sherry and a beer for herself. The beer seemed to provide a certain thread of continuity in the labyrinth into which she had, with slightly less reason than Theseus, plunged. As they resettled themselves in the living room, Kate told Dorinda about that feeling of being in a labyrinth with no thread.

"Ah, but you have a thread; we've given it to you and so probably will Gabrielle when you read what she's written," Dorinda said. "The question no one's answered, certainly not dear old Emmanuel Foxx, is what became of Ariadne after she guided Theseus out of the labyrinth. Isn't it really the question of all wives, the ones who see their husbands through the whole bit, and then get forgotten on Naxos. I often ask myself, who forgot whom?"

"There is a theory that Ariadne went no further because she did not want to lose her inheritance on Cnossus."

"Right. She told him to sail on without her. Oh, she may have had a fling with Dionysus; it hardly matters. By the time she'd seen Theseus fling himself into a boat to sail away, she knew she didn't want to go very far with him. Why bother? And you know that Theseus forgot to hoist the white sail when he neared home, and his father, thinking his son dead, killed himself. My analysis is," Dorinda concluded, sipping her sherry, "that Theseus had this unconscious wish to kill his father: all men's unconscious wishes have to do with killing and triumphing, and Ariadne discovered her unconscious wish to stay within sight of home and be her own person. The only problem for the rest of us is that we haven't any home to stay in sight of, metaphorically speaking; no home of our very own."

167

AMANDA CROSS

"A clever analysis," Kate said. "Do you think that's how Gabrielle saw it?"

"We won't know till we look, till you look, as we all fervently hope you will." Dorinda finished her sherry and held out her glass like a child asking for more. Kate fetched her more sherry, glad of the time to digest all this. Dorinda's mode was clearly now, as it had ever been, fast talking and amusing tales. But, Kate suspected, one made a profound mistake if one underestimated Dorinda, a mistake Kate intended to avoid.

"Do you suppose Gabrielle went back to England in the spirit of Ariadne staying in sight of Cnossus?" Kate asked.

"I wondered about that. We three have a theory." Kate indicated, with absolute truth, that she could hardly wait to hear it.

"I learned from Mark Hansford that Gabrielle's surviving brother, even then tottering happily into old age, went to see her when she moved to London and then again at the nursing home. Mark saw him, but apparently he was anything but forthcoming. Of course, neither were Anne or Nellie or anyone else at that time, but the brother's smoke screen was impenetrable. He's died since, needless to say, so all we have is our theory. Maybe Gabrielle's papers will prove us right or wrong, but if what we think about Gabrielle is true, there won't be anything personal about her or her families either by birth or marriage in her papers. *Our* theory is that, whether or not in imitation of Ariadne, Gabrielle decided to go home to the place where she was born. She wrote to her brother—you understand this is all supposition—and he, with the mellowness that is supposed to come with age and sometimes does, had his manly heart softened and went to see her."

168

"In her place in Kensington?"

"So one assumes. They might have met in Regent's Park or Kensington Gardens or watching the change of the guard at Buckingham Palace ('Christopher Robin went down with Alice'—I tried to read Pooh to my sons but they weren't having any, too out of date), the point is they talked long enough for Gabrielle to gather that wherever home was, it wasn't with that stuffy brother. Probably he wanted her to return to the family mansion and become a proper sister or aunt or whatever seemly female function he had in mind. So it was clear wherever home was, it wasn't at the old homestead or whatever the English call it. I like to think and so does Nellie that she decided home was what she had written, and that's why she got so antsy about preserving it. According to the records as studied and reported by Mark, the brother went to see her again at the nursing home, perhaps to assuage his, I hope, horribly sticky conscience, but she wasn't having any: too far gone. End of my story, ratified by the other two as not unlikely."

"But there isn't a shred of evidence for any of this?"

"Not a shred. It's a reconstruction out of the whole cloth, whatever that means. But I think it has a certain air of verisimilitude, don't you?"

"I haven't a clue, as the English say," Kate said. "Not the smallest thread to follow. But I do like your story. It's both appropriate to the facts and creative. Perhaps that's the best that can be said for any biography when all is said and done."

"Will you work on Gabrielle's, then? Not the kind of biography, a new kind, carrying Gabrielle's writings with it."

"Pure fiction, in fact, like Gabrielle's writings as we are imagining them?"

"But they won't be fiction," Dorinda raised her voice in great excitement. "Surely you can see that. The Gabrielle in all the biographies of the great Emmanuel Foxx and for all we know in Foxx's novel is fiction. What Gabrielle really was will be truly revealed in her writings."

"Always supposing it is writings, and not a lot of gibberish or laundry receipts, or letters Nellie will never let anyone publish." Kate sounded wary, an accurate reflection of her feelings.

"It all depends on what you find. So why not buzz off to England with Anne and settle all our hopes and fears? Will you do that, or have I discouraged you with all my talking? Hilda talked a lot too, I distinctly remember and, anyway, everyone said so. It's the Goddard genes. My father talked unendingly, but always amusingly, give credit where credit is due."

"You're quite amusing yourself," Kate said. "I'm beginning to give a lot of credit to the Goddard genes."

"Well, thank you for those kind words, but don't overdo it. I mean about the Goddard genes. They're running pretty thin these days. My sons, except for the youngest, have none of the famous Goddard charm. The youngest is rather like me, which I noticed the first moment they handed him to me. He had the same doubtful smile. Gas, probably, but that's how it looked at the time." She rose from her chair.

"Might I ask one more question?" Kate said.

"Certainly." Dorinda dropped expectantly back into her chair. "Anything. I was devoted to truth in my murky youth, and I have returned to that mode."

"Why did you mention Sally Seton when we had lunch?"

"Oh, not for any deep reason. Not because I'd ever kissed anyone like Clarissa, though Anne says I did run around the house naked. It was just that, having all those sons and a husband who might be considered the equivalent of a manufacturer in the north of England, and having had a more interesting youth than maturity, I was struck by the resemblance between Lady Rosseter, as Sally became, and me."

"I see," Kate said, disappointed, she hardly knew why.

"No," Dorinda said, "there was more than that. There was the fact that my girlhood was the best part, with Anne and later with Nellie. That for women, there is a time before the need to impress men when women can find a life with each other, a friendship, a companionship, whatever you want to call it. At least, some women have found it; others not. That's certainly part of my Sally Seton persona. May I go now?"

"I may go try to visit your mother again, if she'll have me," Kate said as she walked Dorinda to the door. "Do you think that's a good idea?"

"A splendid idea. Mummy took to you as I knew she would, just as all of us took to you. You'd do Mummy a world of good." And waving as though she were about to embark on some long voyage, perhaps as though from a departing ship, Dorinda waited for the elevator as Kate closed the door.

The same woman in a white dress let Kate into Eleanor's living room. One home I *have* seen, Kate thought, and a good thing too: reading of Anne's and Dorinda's childhood in Eleanor's home, some of it in this very room, transformed Eleanor's living room into a symbol of return. Everything is metaphors and symbols around these three and Gabrielle, Kate thought.

"I'm glad to see you again, my dear," Eleanor said. "I apologize for nodding off on you the last time. It's death, you know, claiming us in the nicest possible way, reminding us the final sleep is not far off." She paused a moment, as though expecting something. "I'm very glad you are not one of those people who insist on bursting forth with pleas of denial if one mentions death, even one as old as I. Dorinda said I would find you a sensible person, knowing that's a great compliment for me after a life with the Goddards, and you are sensible, Dorinda is right. She's been right more often than not lately, I'm pleased to say. Well, I shall try to stick with Gabrielle, which is what I'm sure you want to talk about, before I nod off again."

"I haven't much to ask, if anything," Kate said. "I just felt I wanted to see you again. I so much enjoyed our visit the last time."

"Thank you, my dear. I feel you really mean that. I was hoping you would return, and trying to remember some of the things Gabrielle said during our short chats together, before Emmanuel started again with his imperious demands. I know it's no good my pretending she said something she didn't say. That would be little use to you. She didn't talk much about Foxx's novel, the one called *Ariadne*, though she certainly did indicate that she didn't know what all the fuss was about. She also said once that men thought they understood women—didn't they?—and that Emmanuel thought he was so clever pretending to put a woman at the center of his novel."

"Pretending? Did she say pretending?"

"Oh, yes, quite definitely. Because Ariadne wasn't at

the center, Gabrielle said, she was just an excuse for men showing off. I remember something else now. Isn't it funny how once you start talking, other things come back? She told me one of those times that she had tried to read James Joyce's *Ulysses*, since that was supposed to be the great competitor for the-greatest-novel-ever-written-in-the-twentieth-century stakes, and that while she couldn't understand most of it, she rather took to Leopold Bloom and thought that if Joyce didn't put a woman at the center, he at least put a man there who didn't think he was a god. I quite agreed with her.''

''It sounds a bit as though she resented Foxx's fame.''

''Oh, no; then I've given you the wrong impression. You see, she soon spotted me as someone whose place in the family I'd married into was comparable to her place, and so she admitted a few things she would never have said to anyone else.''

''Not to mention,'' Kate interjected, ''that you are the sort of person to whom people tell what they tell to no one else.''

''Well, one of the advantages in being a calm person in a very volatile family is that you seem sensible; most of the time, I was merely bewildered. But I'm sure you mustn't get the idea that Gabrielle ever breathed a word against Emmanuel, at least not often. She must have known when she ran off with him that he was the sort of man people make a great fuss over. He thought he was a genius, he was a genius, and she didn't try to undermine that in any way. But she must have wanted to be her own person once in a while, and that was rarely possible.''

''Did you ever want to be your own person?'' Kate rather daringly asked.

"The truth is, I never had much time to think about that. All the early years were spent trying not to be bowled over. When I finally got some confidence, our life was so busy I never thought much about myself, except how to dress and make arrangements; dealing with Sig and Dorinda was a full-time occupation just to begin with. The idea of being my own person only became possible as an idea or a reality after Sig died. And then I took a long time about it. But I do think I had the chance to be my own person then. I often wonder if Gabrielle did; I like to think she did, after Emmanuel died, I mean. And being my own person as well as a friend to Dorinda has been quite heady."

It was a long speech, and Kate could see Eleanor beginning to tire. Her having returned to talking of Dorinda was, in its way, a confession of weariness. Kate rose to go. She sensed that this time, Eleanor would like her to leave while she was still awake and herself—her own person, not, even momentarily, in the hands of death or anyone else.

Kate said good-bye to her with more feeling than she had remembered having experienced at a farewell. It was not sorrow; one could not sorrow for the quick, kind death of a woman this old. She had kept her wits and, with equal good fortune, might slip quickly and easily into death. Kate wished they had met sooner. Having got to know Eleanor would not be the least of the benefits she had accrued in her pursuit of Gabrielle.

Kate said her farewells, and let herself out of the apartment, Eleanor waving gently to her until the door closed.

Nine

KATE had been looking into London hotels in a desultory manner, when Anne called to say she had been lent a house in Highgate which she, at least, would occupy for three weeks; Kate could stay as long as she liked. Also there was a cat and a garden, both of which Anne would look to; she did hope that Kate had no horror of cats.

Kate did not, rather liked them, in fact, when casually met. But did Anne know the owner and had she seen the house?

Oh, yes, Anne had stayed there before, it was really quite nice, with two floors and two bathrooms, though a *very* unmodern kitchen. Still, they could eat out. The only drawback was an odd one: the insurance company insisted that each time before the occupants went out they lock the doors to each room. This was a dreadful nuisance, but Anne had agreed to comply with this condition now as in the past.

Personally, she doubted that anyone else bothered, but her friend was a stickler in these matters.

What, Kate asked, did the friend do besides live in a nice house in Highgate?

She was a singer, in opera, concerts, recitals, and also played the French horn. Anne was sure Kate would like her though of course they would not meet except to say hello and good-bye.

Did the friend know anything about Gabrielle?

Nothing; Anne had never mentioned it.

All that needed to be settled, then, was the date and time of their flight; their arrival had to be synchronized with the departure of Anne's friend, so they had to time it closely. That is, the friend needed only to hand over the keys and, if Anne knew her, repeat all the instructions about the garden, the cat, the dates of trash pickup, and locking the inner doors. She was a wonderful person, Anne's friend, but, as Anne had said, a stickler. They would, however, be comfortable and have plenty of space in which to contemplate Gabrielle's papers. There was a bus to the center of London, stores not too far away, and a fine pub in nearby Hampstead, useful if Kate liked English beer, ploughman's lunch, and cheese and pickle sandwiches as much as Anne did. Kate said that she did, and was even known to relish a Scotch egg.

Arriving at Heathrow after a not-too-terrible night flight and finding that, for once, the airport workers were not on strike and the airport buses were running, Kate and Anne arrived at Victoria Station and there took a taxi to Highgate. Kate had always ardently admired London taxicabs; in these black high vehicles Kate came as close, she told Anne, to feeling like a queen as she was ever likely to under any circumstances.

Anne's friend was waiting for them, and flung open the door with a great shout of welcome. She was in her middle sixties like Anne, and like Anne had the great energy and exuberance that, Kate thought, we tend to identify exclusively with youth; probably she had expected a younger person because of the French horn. Kate liked her immediately. Everything about her, as she led them rapidly through the house reeling off instructions and advocating the delights and conveniences of the neighborhood, including the graves of Marx and George Eliot, was delightful. Having imparted her information, and having announced that her bags were already stashed in the car, she backed it out of the tiny garage and steamed off.

"The last time I stayed here," Anne said as they stood in the dining room admiring the garden and feeling rather bewildered, "there was a block celebration for the Queen Mum's birthday. They took the electricity they needed from this house, and it really was quite marvelous, as rock-and-rolly as anything in America, with flashing lights and all. I think it was rock and roll, anyway it was loud, and Lavinia, my friend, stuck cotton in her ears. I'm not very good at distinguishing contemporary popular music and I don't suppose you are either."

"Certainly not," Kate said. "Aging without children one tends to ignore popular music, let alone the shifts from one mode to the next. When I hum I hum the Beatles or Simon and Garfunkel from the days when I did notice popular music. Shall we go and get the papers today? I suppose instead of acting madly eager, I ought to assume a mien of quiet patience, but that's beyond my capabilities. I'm madly eager."

"I'll call the bank," Anne said. "I've already written. We better get some bags to collect the papers in. I kept Gabrielle's sacks as you know and took them back to America, but it seemed rather perverse to drag them back again across the ocean. Besides, they're decades old, if I shouldn't speak of half-centuries, and might fall apart at the worst possible moment. Would you rather sleep upstairs or down?"

Kate chose up because it made her feel more like being in a house, which she wasn't very often. She mentioned this to Anne.

"I often dream of having a house," Anne said. "Not like this, with more land and off somewhere. But I know perfectly well I would die of the isolation in a month, after the fun of settling in was over. I think Gabrielle may have had some such dream when she came back to England, but she saw the errors of that way and settled for rooms in Kensington. Are you one of the rare persons who does not dream of a rural retreat?"

"I am, however rare. I'm a city person, but this house does seem to offer the best of both worlds, especially if you like gardening. I'm afraid I can't identify anything but a rose and a pansy. Shall we have much to do in the garden?"

"No. Not this time of year. I'll do it. You can concentrate on finding restaurants for us to dally in."

"Did you eat in restaurants when you were last here?"

"No, but then I wasn't here alone; besides being a vegetarian, Lavinia eats very modestly. I went to Selfridge's incredible food floor one day and bought cheeses and other goodies, and we ate those with bread and crackers I picked up around here. Lavinia makes her own wine too, which is really quite tasty.''

"Well, let's us do the same, except for pubs," Kate said. "Pubs for lunch and cheese for supper; we shall do very well. Now do call the bank before they decide to close on us. I'll unpack." And Kate, grabbing her suitcase, marched happily upstairs where Anne, as she prepared to telephone, could hear her tramping about and exclaiming with delight.

When she spoke to the proper person at the bank, a man with a quite dignified manner on the phone, she was informed that she could come tomorrow to collect the belongings from her vault, that she would need several items of identification with photograph, and that she might ask for him in person. They would be happy if she had brought some of their past invoices with her to show by way of further identification.

"One would think it was jewels," Anne said. "Gabrielle's papers may be worth more to me and even the world, but they do make me feel as though I should bring along an armed guard. Well, I am bringing you."

The next morning they set out for Archway Road where they caught the bus for London. At Kate's request, they climbed to the upper deck (smoking allowed) and watched the streets and houses as they passed—Kentish Town, Camden Town, ending up near the Charing Cross Road. They walked to Oxford Street, where at Marks and Spencer they purchased two bags, sufficient, Anne thought, to hold all the papers.

"Perhaps we should get a third, just in case," Kate said, suddenly worried about not being able to carry off all the papers at once, or having to crush and perhaps crumble them by packing them too tightly.

179

Kate could not quite subdue the sensation of being involved in some sort of secret plan, some undercover plot to fool the other side, whoever they might be. Could there be any two people on a mission arousing less interest in the populace, general, criminal, or subversive? Really, she thought, looking at Anne and herself when they had paid for the bags and were leaving the store, one could hardly find two less provocative individuals if one worked at it with both hands for a fortnight.

Kate thought the bank people looked a little startled at their entrance encumbered with large, obviously empty bags, but Anne, putting on her executive manner, asked for the man she had talked to yesterday, and sat down to wait. Kate wondered if anticipation was as clearly written on her face as on Anne's. Probably. Excitement was to be expected if one was redeeming what had been put away in such a dramatic fashion and with such an apparent need for haste those many years ago. Anne had written that she felt then as though the Gestapo were on her trail; now they again felt somewhat the same sensation. Perhaps, Kate thought, we live in a world where it comes naturally to think of ourselves as spies. Yet spies implied betrayal, and here there was no betrayal. Or was that the whole point, that there had been? That Gabrielle had been betrayed, and her name was about to be cleared; her name, that is, as a separate person and not the wife-of-a-famous-writer.

They did not wait long. The bank manager, or whoever he was, the man in charge of vaults perhaps, invited them into his office, examined Anne's papers and identification with great care, and then prepared to lead them downward to the vault area. Clearly, he had taken Anne at face value; a sixty-year-old woman, more or less, had to be herself, unless she was pretending to be another sixty-year-old woman, which would have required more extensive accumulation of false documents than this man found it possible to attribute to Anne. But why am I so aware of fraud? Kate wondered. It is all straightforward now. Either the papers will be wonderful or they will be a total loss. That was all there was to it.

The vault was a large one, just as Anne had said it was. It must have cost a pretty penny to maintain all these years, and Kate wondered if Gabrielle had thought of that. Perhaps she didn't expect that the papers would remain so long sequestered in expensive quarters.

"I'm surprised you didn't decide to remove them long before this," Kate said to Anne as they awaited the man's long process with keys and forms.

"But I never wanted to think of all that again. It was a new life I was starting, a life in which Dorinda and all her connections, famous or not, were to have no part. After I left the bank, and learned that Gabrielle had gone to the hospital, after I cabled Eleanor, I went into a decline, collapsed in a heap, sank into a kind of trough: honestly, I don't know how to explain it, but somehow it became clear to me that I had to begin living as Anne Gringold, and not as a ghost still haunting the Goddards, the Foxxes, and the Jersey shore.

"I had been frightened. I don't know why, but I had been. And I could tell no one. So I decided upon the only therapy that occurred to me: an absolutely clean break. Oh, I went to visit Gabrielle, as you know, but she was gone from this world and so, in a sense, was I. Apart from paying the bank's charges I no longer thought at all of my childhood. It was only when I wrote my memoir that I was able to speak of the papers and to begin thinking again about the past. That, of course, was after I talked to Eleanor. I'm glad now I got the whole thing down on paper and began to remember such a vital part of my history again. But in between there had to be a time when I lived a wholly other life, wholly as myself.''

Then the man and his assistant had the vault open, and the papers lay there, piled up, starting to yellow around the edges but not yet, Kate was glad to see, brittle. She held one of the sheets up to the light, looking for the watermark, and saw that Gabrielle had used 100 percent rag paper; either that was what was sold her, or she had some sense of preserving her work. Perhaps that was the kind of paper Foxx wrote on, so she did too, particularly. if she decided that her manuscript, because unpublished, had to last at least as long as his.

It took some time to move all the papers out of the vault, laying them down neatly, keeping them in the same order, not crushing or folding them in the bags. As Anne pointed out, the papers had probably not been in any particular order when she locked them away, so that it was unlikely that they were now going to be easily sorted. Indeed, it might take days, weeks, to get them into any proper order, if indeed an order could be discovered. For all that, Kate felt rather as Donald Johanson did when he found the fossilized bones of the earliest hominid, whom he would name Lucy: Perhaps once in a very few lifetimes a person is privileged to come upon a discovery that will shift some established and widely held view, that will, in its own way, transform human knowledge. Kate felt that this was such a moment, and she had time to wonder how odd it was that this should have happened to her of all people, and exactly in this way.

When the papers were all packed away (and they had had, after all, to use the third bag Kate had insisted on) the bags became remarkably heavy: paper is no lightweight. Several of the men in the bank helped Anne and Kate to carry the load to the street and commandeer a taxi—a real London taxi, as Kate remarked with relief.

The driver was a woman which seemed, as did everything on this fateful day, to be significant, as though they were all in a film someone was making, and the decision to have a woman driver had been reached, logically, after extended conferences. The driver was both pleasant and accommodating, and helped them lug the bags into the house in Highgate when they had arrived. Kate offered her a cool drink while Anne stood over the bags as though they might walk away if she took her eye off them; the driver accepted a glass of water (fortunately, since Anne's friend did not approve of commercial soft drinks) and seemed pleased with her large tip. So far so good.

Anne unlocked the door to the sitting room and they dragged the bags in there. The dining room may have had the advantage of a large table on which to work, but it also had French windows leading out to the garden which suddenly seemed perilous, and besides, they needed somewhere to eat. Moving all the furniture back against the walls, they made themselves comfortable on the floor and began to unpack the bags, putting the papers in arbitrary piles but sneaking occasional looks to see if any pattern presented itself. Anne said she remembered feeling this way when she and Dorinda waited for Nellie's first arrival. Kate could not remember ever having felt quite this way before. The moment resembled other moments of joy or achievement or passion, resembled but was far from the same. And when, Kate thought, did I last crawl around a floor like someone laying tiles?

"It's a novel," Anne said, who had been looking at the sheets of paper more closely than Kate. "It's got dialogue, and people have names, and places are described. Look here: see what I mean?"

Kate crawled to Anne's side of the floor and looked. She read a page, and then picked up other pages from other piles, moving, amazed, from one pile to the other, reading pages from all of them. Suddenly she found herself wishing Reed could be there now, lounging in one of the pushed-back chairs with his long legs stretched out, sharing her excitement and delight. But there was only Anne.

She sat back on her heels. "It's a novel all right," Kate said. "It's another *Ariadne*. The characters have the same names, it takes place in the same scenes, at least as far as I can tell, but it's altogether different. Look, it has the same first sentence: page one, chapter one. 'He is coming tonight, she thought; one more day of waiting.' "

"I haven't read Foxx's novel since we were kids," Anne said. "Maybe I better run out and buy a copy."

"Let's first see what order we can find by the page numbers."

They scrambled for a time among the piles, soon reaching the same sad conclusion. "She's numbered each chapter beginning again with page one," Anne said. "You know that was the beginning because it said chapter one, page one, but if we find a page six there isn't a clue as to which chapter it belongs to. Why couldn't she have put the chapter number with each page number or have sensibly numbered all the pages in sequence?"

It was a rhetorical question, but Kate answered it. "I think she probably wrote one chapter at a time, in stolen, secret moments. She'd probably hidden the rest of the manuscript away somewhere. She probably didn't remember how many pages she'd already written. Maybe we had better get a copy of Foxx's *Ariadne;* since it was clearly the scaffolding on which she wrote her novel, it might give us a clue as to which chapter we've got a page of as we go through the papers. Anyway, it's better than not having any guide at all."

"Somehow I think she'd be horrified to know we based her papers on Foxx's work."

"Then she should have ordered them better," Kate said with some asperity. "Besides, I rather think she must have meant this to be read as an answer to Foxx's novel. Perhaps that was the whole point. Wasn't she writing Foxx's novel as she thought it ought to be written?"

"You're probably right; but do you think she modeled every chapter on his, all in the same order? Mightn't the scenes or the order of events be something she would want to change?"

"Yes," Kate said, "it might. But I still think we better start with Foxx's novel, since I can't think of anywhere else to begin. Can you?"

"No," Anne said. "Let's walk over to the bookstore in Hampstead and buy *Ariadne*. It's bound to be in Penguin or something. We can even stop at a pub and celebrate. Although I do feel some trepidation at leaving all her work just lying here."

"We'll lock the living-room door, as we promised," Kate said, "and we won't be gone long." While she was speaking, the cat, who had up to now ignored them except for allowing them to let her in and out and provide meals, came into the room and, after a certain amount of reconnoitering, settled down on a stack of papers. "She'll watch them for us," Kate said.

"It'll mean locking her in here with them."

"Well," Kate said as they stood at the living-room door, we'll give her a chance to leave if she wants to. "Come on pussens," Kate said, holding the door open, shutting it to declare her intentions, and then holding it open again. "Do you want to stay or leave?"

The cat rearranged herself on her stack of papers, and closed her eyes. "Stay," Kate said. Anne locked the door, they locked the outer door and set off for Hampstead.

This was, Kate realized, one of those days when everything would work. The bookstore had a copy of *Ariadne*. There were days like that, there was no explaining them, they were a miracle, just as there were days when nothing went right. Life was like that, after all, Kate thought, even if we don't choose to make too much of it and risk sounding like solitary solipsists or believers in an ordained personal destiny.

"Come on," Kate said. "Let's get that celebratory drink."

"I'm worried about the papers," Anne said, obviously recognizing a certain irrationality in the remark.

"I know; so am I. But we have to conquer that. We can't stand guard over them day and night. Look at it this way; if a thief did break in, the papers would be the last thing he'd want."

"He might be cold and use them to light a fire."

"What we need," Kate said, "is a drink."

*   *   *

The task before them, even after the reassurance of cheese and pickle sandwiches washed down with the best English ale, was overwhelming. They had hundreds of pages, with no clue as to which page numbers went in which chapters.

"There is only one way to begin," Kate said.

"Read Emmanuel Foxx's beastly novel, I suppose," Anne retorted.

"Even before that. We have to make stacks of all the pages of the same numbers. Then, when we've got all the page ones together, all the page twos together, and so on, we shall have to decide which page one goes with which page two . . ."

"And so on."

"Exactly. Let's begin with the page-one pile over here."

"If you say so," Anne muttered. "I thought I was supposed to be the one with the business sense and the orderly mind."

"You are," Kate said. "This requires an enthusiasm more appropriate to nursery games. Look, after we've decided where each pile is to go, preferably in numerical order since any order, however elementary, is welcome, you call out the pages and I'll run around and put them each in its proper pile. Does that sound okay?"

"It sounds exhausting but inevitable." Anne lowered herself to the floor, and pulled a stack of papers toward her. "I'm ready when you are," she said.

"Okay. I've got the places for piles over here," Kate said, meanwhile stacking all the papers as near to Anne as she could get them. "You could sit in a chair and bend over, you know."

"No. If I'm going to be bending down all the time, I might as well start down. Less wear and tear on the lower back, though rather more on the thighs," she added as she leaned from a sitting position to move some papers. "Ready? Let's go."

The following hours were hectic; Anne and Kate resembled nothing so much as two rather dotty dames engaged in some sort of witchlike maneuver. Anne would call out a number: "eighteen" for example. Kate would grab the page, rush over to the stack designated "eighteen," and add the page to it, written side up. They got quite good at it, and really developed what to Kate seemed a remarkable performance of speed and coordination. But after hours of this, she began to feel that if she bent over one more time her back might well refuse ever to straighten up again. She suggested a walk, a return to the pub, and refreshment.

"Would you prefer tea? It's almost time," Kate said to Anne. "Scones and jam and a fine upper-class English repast?"

"I think I would prefer steak and kidney pie, beer, and a fine working-class English repast, if it's all the same to you."

"Preferable to me," Kate said, "though I fear the Hampstead pub is no more working class than we are. Still, it beats tea." And once again locking up the rooms, leaving the cat this time in the garden, they set out. Kate suggested that they go by way of the bookstore, as there were several other books she wanted to buy.

"You can't be thinking of reading anything to do with anything else, can you?" Anne asked.

"Of course not," Kate said. "Silly question." In the bookstore, she equipped herself with Joseph Campbell's *The Masks of God*, the volume on Occidental Mythology, and a book she found on the secondhand shelf, proving yet again the day to be one of serendipity and all other good fortune: *The Find of a Lifetime: Sir Arthur Evans and the Discovery of Knossos,* by Sylvia L. Horwitz. Thus armed, and with Anne carrying Foxx's novel, of which they planned to make an outline, they proceeded to the pub.

When they returned, considerably refreshed and reinvigorated, they devoted a few more hours to their page-sorting task, and then, over a nightcap, sketched a rough outline of Foxx's chapters in *Ariadne*. At midnight they separated, Anne to sleep—she was used to early mornings and early nights—and Kate, who seldom slept before one A.M. or rose before nine A.M. if she could help it, to contemplation of the two books she had just purchased for references to Crete, Cnossus, Minoan civilization, for it seemed to be called one of those things. Although there was no way Gabrielle could have read either of the books, since both were published after her death, Kate was certain that in helping Foxx with *his* research, if for no other reason, Gabrielle had learned a good deal about the culture from which Ariadne came. For one thing, Evans's discovery of Cnossus was big news for years, and his book *The Palace of Minos,* as well as the archaeological revelations that preceded it, must have had a great influence on Foxx in the years when he was writing *Ariadne*.

By the next morning Kate had culled two quotations for Anne's perusal, one longish one from Campbell, and one very short one from Sylvia Horwitz. "Start with Campbell," Kate said, handing the book to her with the sentences marked off. "First is a quotation from Martin Nilsson about the Minoan religion. The second and third are Campbell himself; all of these points, however, are from Evans and the substance, if not these exact words, would have been

189

known to Foxx, who chose not to notice them, and to Gabrielle, who (and this is my point) *did* notice them:''

I

"In spite of the limitations imposed by the nature of the evidence, certain characteristic traits of Minoan religion do emerge in contrast to the Greek. . . . And the observation must finally be added that all reference to sexual life, all phallic symbols, such as abound and are so aggressive in numerous religions—including the historic religion of Greece—are in Minoan art completely missing.''

II

"The culture, as many have noted, was apparently of a matriarchal type. The grace and elegance of the ladies in their beautifully flounced skirts, generous decolleté, pretty coiffures, and gay bandeaux, mixing freely with the men, in the courts, in the bull ring—lovely, vivid, and vivacious, gesticulating, chattering, even donning masculine athletic belts to go somersaulting dangerously over the horns and backs of bulls—represent a civilized refinement that has not been often equalled since.''

III

"There were no walled cities in Crete before the coming of the Greeks. There is little evidence of weapons. Battle scenes of kingly conquest play no role in the setting of the style. The tone is of general luxury and delight, a broad participation by all classes in a genial atmosphere of well-being, and the vast development of a profitable commerce by sea, to every port of the archaic world and even—boldly—to regions far beyond.''

"I begin to get your drift," Anne said. "And what does Sylvia Horwitz have to add? I don't mean to sound impatient with your scholarship, but hadn't we better get to sorting the pages?"

"Certainly. This is just one sentence about Evans. I'll read it to you: 'However, [Evans] noted, it was more likely that the fabled labyrinth got its name from the word *labrys*, or double axe, the symbolic weapon of the Minoan Mother Goddess.' "

"Fascinating. Are you planning to provide us with a double ax for the job ahead? I don't mean to sound impatient, Kate, but even if the double ax were a two-edged sword, we'd still have to get the damned pages into some sort of order."

"True. Back to work, as you so wisely suggest. All I'm trying to point out in my tedious way is that the Greeks turned Crete from a matriarchal to a patriarchal culture, not only in fact but in memory. They rewrote its history, which is to say its myths. We may be able to figure out the order of Gabrielle's pages if we have a clue, a thread if you'll excuse the expression, through the labyrinth of her ideas."

"Which is no longer a labyrinth but a double ax."

"And which probably never was a labyrinth in Foxx's sense, but rather a clue to a nature and culture unknown to patriarchal Greece. I don't necessarily believe a word of this, you understand, but I think we must recognize what was being said after Evans's great discovery at Cnossus."

"And what was the Minotaur, then, a Greek interpretation of something or other, like what for instance?"

191

"The suggestion seems to be that the 'bull' gods were the consorts of the queens of Cnossus, and the whole story about Pasiphaë was just another male version of making women either monsters of lust or pure queens of heaven."

"If you say so," Anne said. "How about sorting pages; I'm beginning to think you academics would rather sit around talking than actually do anything."

"Of course," Kate said. "What else is life for? All right, I'm coming. If you will just let me quote John Maynard Keynes, I promise to work silently and with great diligence until ordered to stop."

"Oh, God," Anne sighed. "All right." She leaned dramatically back in her chair—they were still around the breakfast table and the garden, like Kate's ideas, seemed to summon them to less arduous work—and smiled to lift the sting from her words.

"Keynes said," Kate quoted, staring at the ceiling, " 'Both when they are right and when they are wrong, [ideas] are more powerful than is commonly understood. Indeed the world is ruled by little else. Practical men, who believe themselves to be exempt from any intellectual influences, are usually the slaves of some defunct economist.' "

"I'll think about it," Anne said crisply, rising to her feet. "Pages first, ideas and double axes later. Not," she added, patting Kate encouragingly on the shoulder, "that I don't admit your ideas, or Evans's or Campbell's or even Keynes's, may prove exactly the clue we need in the end."

They worked through the hours, reading to each other from pages, trying to sort out the chapters, recognizing Foxx's order and, where it seemed in any way appropriate, following it. Kate could not be constrained altogether from making comments and tossing out observations—such as that it was too bad that Gabrielle had felt the need to follow Foxx's order, but doubtless when one was reinventing one had to build on what was there, as the Greeks had built on and reinvented the myths and stories of Crete—but Anne, torn between ignoring Kate and bawling her out, finally agreed to allow her one comment per hour when they took time out to lie down flat on the floor, stretching and relaxing their aching backs. Kate agreed to this stringency, saying she found the discipline of being allowed only one remark an hour salutary.

Their progress was slow, dogged, and discouraging. They were weary, besieged by shooting pains, and visited by the gremlins who attack those engaged in long and arduous tasks with doubts of their having any value or being in any way worth the effort. But by the end of a week's persistent work, with lunch ignored and dinner each evening at the pub until they both announced themselves unable ever again to contemplate a Scotch egg, they declared their task, in its first stage, complete. Before them, on the sitting-room floor, once they could summon the energy to read it, was at least an approximation of Gabrielle's cherished writings.

Ten

"**Y**OU read it through to yourself," Anne said. "You're the one who's going to have to edit it."

It was the morning after the last page had been tentatively assigned to a chapter, and the chapters put in what seemed a probable order. Nothing was certain, but Kate felt some confidence that they had come close to a reconstruction of Gabrielle's novel. For yes, clearly, it was a novel.

"I could read it to you," Kate suggested, "and we could both decide on whether or not we find the story coherent. Or you could read it to me; or we could read it to each other."

"I'll leave it to you now, if you don't mind," Anne said, staring into the garden. "That is, if you have accepted the editing job together with the writing of the biographical portrait. I know it must seem odd to you, my not being more curious after all this work, but I have a strong sense of wanting to hand it over to you and let you cope. I want to quit thinking about it now. I look forward with great eagerness to reading the book when it emerges, but I really don't want to deal with it anymore. No doubt a psychologist could tell me why if I really cared to know, but I don't. I hope I haven't offended you.''

''No offense in the world,'' Kate said. Strangely enough, she understood Anne's feelings without understanding why, a case of muddled conviction. ''But before I fly home with the manuscript, leaving you to have a decent vacation in this nice house, there is one more task I need your help with.'' The cat was sitting before the French windows, blinking in the sun, and there seemed promise of good times to be had here without the endless shuffling of papers.

''What task?''

''We need to make copies,'' Kate said, patting the stack of papers beside her. ''The thought of losing this or, worse, having to start sorting again, is not to be contemplated.''

''Probably the English have copying shops the way we do.''

''Probably, but we can't use them. We've got to do this ourselves, by hand.''

''Are you planning to buy your own copying machine and leave it as a house present for Lavinia?''

''If we have to. I rather thought of calling Reed and asking him to locate a law office in London with a copying machine which we might use on Saturday or Sunday. I did think of asking Simon Pearlstine to ask a publisher or agent here for the favor, but I realized I don't want to explain to Simon on a transatlantic basis what it is I'm copying and what has happened to his cherished idea of a biography. That sort of thing goes down better face-to-face and with the material to hand. Will you help with the copying?''

"I can't think of a reason to refuse, though I would if I could. How many copies do you want to make and what do you plan to do with them?"

"I've gathered you'd rather not have Gabrielle's papers, even photocopied, on your hands at this point. I don't know why but I have the sense that you've made the right decision. That means that I shall keep one copy, mail one copy to myself in New York, send one copy by some other means to another address (yet to be determined) in New York, and leave the original here with a law firm or again in a bank, whatever Reed advises. I'm rather into taking advice at this moment, and, as you can see, I'm doubling my protection, outwitting even the most malevolent intentions of ill chance. Also, I'm sure Reed will feel as I do that the original belongs here, at least until you and Nellie decide what to do with it. It may, if the publication of Gabrielle's novel is a success, bring quite a bit of money when auctioned off."

"I know," Anne said. "You're scattering so many copies because you don't wish to give the gods any chance to do easy mischief. That doesn't sound any more bonkers to me than to you."

Anne smiled, and Kate knew it was going to be all right, that she and Anne were still on the same side, that Anne was still a friend and likely to remain so. So Kate went off to consult Reed by long distance, and to ask him, as she liked to put it, to pull strings to get her what she wanted. Reed had often pointed out that he didn't pull strings, he called in favors, but Kate found that view of things uncongenial. She knew, nonetheless, that Reed was good to people, generous with his help, and many considered it a pleasure to help him in his turn, even for the sake of his nosey-Parker wife.

* * *

Reed's strings were as effective as ever. He found a law firm willing to lend out its photocopying machine and happy to keep in safety the original manuscript once a copy had been made. He suggested a New York law firm to whom a copy might be sent, and urged Kate to carry the remaining copy home with her on the airplane, contemplating it the while. He would meet her at JFK Airport when instructed about her flight. He looked forward to seeing her very soon. "Mutual," Kate assured him, wanting very much to get all this over, to go home to Reed and a life that had come to seem charmingly calm and sane, with most of its activities not taking place on the floor.

Meanwhile, she and Anne trundled off late the next afternoon, each of them carrying half the manuscript with the wonderfully mad conviction that if one was run over, at least half of Gabrielle's endeavors would survive, unbloodied, unscattered. Kate had been told by older colleagues of the days when there was no photocopying at all, and the single typescript of a precious dissertation, representing perhaps a decade's work, would be carted about by its frenzied creator. One might have made a carbon copy, but, too often, one hadn't. Those were indeed parlous times, here repeated at least for a few hours more. After tedious hours of feeding Gabrielle's pages into the copying machine, Kate would be ready to leave London and Anne to their mutual enjoyment.

But at the last minute, a reprieve marvelously presented itself, first in the form of an English lawyer who knew and admired Reed, was delighted to meet Kate, honored to meet Anne, eager to be helpful. He had work and would remain in his office until they finished: he would then see to the proper stowing away of the original manuscript. Meanwhile, the copy machine operator, Mr. Martin, known to all as Phil, was here to help them feed the pages into the modern copier which not only could make four copies at a time but could collate and staple them into the bargain.

The expressions of both Kate and Anne, who had been beaming with gratitude, changed to alarmed apprehension. Telling Reed about it afterward, Kate saw how funny their two horrified expressions must have been, but at the time she and Anne feared, sharply and simultaneously, Phil Martin's chance to read Gabrielle's words. The English lawyer, whose name they had in their anxiety missed the first time and felt unable, from awkwardness, to have repeated, sensed the reason for their alarm. He ushered them into this office, each of them still hugging to her chest her half of the manuscript, and shut the door.

"Don't worry about Phil's having any interest in your manuscript," he said. "Phil wouldn't be interested unless it were about a soccer game or a rock group and probably not even then. He's happy to make overtime staying to help you, but you probably couldn't pay him to read a word of what you have there, and between us, I'm not even sure that he could read much of it. Phil's got a knack with machines, but for him the written language is something that had its place only in antediluvian times. If it isn't electronic, mechanical, or athletic, Phil doesn't trouble with it. Anyway, you can stay there with him while he makes his copies, and grab each sheet of the original as he removes it, if that will make you happy."

"You must wonder what this is all about," Kate said. After all, he was an associate, perhaps a friend, of Reed's, and one might be well advised to stop being the nervous editor and become a civilized woman and professor.

"Reed told me enough to let me know what we are copying and keeping," the lawyer said. "Go and have it copied, and I'll be waiting here for the original when you're done. Perhaps you would both like to have dinner with me?"

"How kind," Kate said, glancing over at Anne who shook her head. "I have to make a plane early tomorrow and Anne is rather tired, as we both are. But thank you for asking."

And they returned to Phil, impatiently awaiting their task which was keeping him after hours, however well paid. Kate and Anne placed the manuscript in proper order near to him—they had by now tentatively numbered the pages from beginning to end—and watched him work with a speed and efficiency that was quite breathtaking. Before their eyes, Gabrielle's precious papers were transformed to something now readily available to anyone, now somehow part of the permanent record of the twentieth century's last decade.

Phil was careful, but once he grabbed a sheet a bit roughly, and they heard it slightly tear; they both gasped as though he had struck them. "Easy does it, love," he said in an extraordinary accent but with a certain kindness. Clearly, he thought them two mad biddies, one old, the other getting there, carrying on about a heap of paper as though it were real money. Phil shrugged. Women much over the age of twenty held neither interest nor possibility for him: you paid him, he did his job, and on to the real world.

He finished with amazing speed. Anne had brought mailing envelopes for the copies destined for New York, one via the post office, the other via Kate. The original was carefully wrapped and handed over to the nice English lawyer, in whose office they made their farewells. Kate once again clutched her copy to her chest, but with less anxiety. They thanked the lawyer profusely, relief rendering their gratitude near to fulsome, and departed into the London evening.

The first phase in the resurrection of Gabrielle's papers was finished. Kate wondered if she had pictured it this way, not the copying machine, of course, but the first stages of the journey to publication. Anne, upon being asked, said she had imagined Gabrielle there the whole time Phil was carrying on, in spirit of course.

"Of course," Kate said, hailing a taxi which, by a miracle, was depositing a customer near them. After stowing their copies in the house and letting the cat out, they walked around for a final drink together at "their" Hampstead pub. Kate had offered a proper restaurant dinner, but Anne wanted to stick with the by-now-familiar routine, and Kate agreed with her. It would, in any case, be a considerable time before Kate ate another steak and kidney pie, to say nothing of a glass of bitter.

As Kate and Anne drank and were having their final pub meal together, the London lawyer called Reed, catching him about to retire, to report that all had gone well, they would guard the manuscript with their lives, but Kate had not quite been as anticipated. She seemed quiet, nervous, not at all the sort of person he had been led to expect, didn't look as though she would say boo to a goose.

"She's never been in charge of an original manuscript before," Reed said, laughing. "You must have dinner with us when next you're in New York and meet her in her true form. It's worth a transatlantic flight, I assure you."

"It's a date," the English lawyer said, practicing his Americanese.

* * *

Kate treated herself to a first-class seat on her return. Sitting like a baby in a high chair, usually in alarming proximity to some overweight neighbor, had lost its appeal; she had also lost her faith in sufficiently light traffic to permit her to sleep in three adjoining seats, as on the outward journey. Alone, she relaxed and enjoyed the pleasant service, accepting a glass of champagne as they awaited the flight.

"To Gabrielle," she said, startling the stewardess, to whom she explained that this was a toast rather than a request or comment. The stewardess smiled, but Kate noticed her saying something to the steward, who served her from then on out. I must be turning into a typical batty traveler, she thought with some pleasure. So long as they left her to herself, she didn't mind.

Well before the airplane had filled up, taxied into the runway line and been assigned its order for takeoff, Kate had settled down with Gabrielle's novel. She had adamantly restrained herself from any judgment, any careful contemplation of the novel, while she was in London, preferring to keep her attention on the physical task at hand. She would have to decide about the edition—whether or not she wanted to do it—and she would have to decide what to say to Simon Pearlstine. It was possible to imagine both delight and dismay as his logical reaction, and Kate wanted to be certain of her ground before she even broached the subject with him.

Kate contemplated the top page of Gabrielle's manuscript: "He is coming tonight, she thought; one more day of waiting," read the opening sentence, the first sentence now of both Emmanuel's and Gabrielle's novels. But while Emmanuel's first sentence had indicated anticipation, eagerness, a wild desire, Gabrielle's rendition of her heroine's thought was ironic, fearful, and desperate. The intruder was about to appear. Ariadne, as Foxx's Artemisia was called in the beginning of Gabrielle's novel, had been advised by Daedalus to give Theseus, when he should come, the thread of the labyrinth; he would then kill the Minotaur but not, it was to be hoped, her or her mother or sister. Greek men were violent: rapists, triumphant over women and weaker men whenever possible. Thwarted, Theseus might kill her whole family, seize the holy double ax, and murder everyone along with the Minotaur. Her only chance was to appear to have anticipated, with the fullest possible girlish glee, his coming. This was the only chance of escape, for her, for her mother, Pasiphaë, her sister, Phaedre, and the priestesses.

"I thought the labyrinth was a double ax, the sign of the priestesses of Crete, and therefore not a labyrinth at all," Kate muttered, inviting a quick glance from the steward and confirming his worst fears. Kate laughed to herself. I am becoming dotty, she said. Gabrielle's influence. I must try and collect myself before we arrive.

Her question was soon cleared up: the labyrinth was the whole palace of Cnossus. That was how it was built, and the famous dance floor and place of acrobatics over the horns of bulls were all part of the labyrinth, part of the palace, all in the shape of the double-sided ax. Kate admired the skill with which Gabrielle embodied this in the novel: she must have read every morsel by Evans about his discoveries of the ancient Cretan civilization.

Her Crete was a civilization that feared the violence and brutality of foreign men. Crete was a matriarchy in the sense that the priests and the queen were women; but its men flourished as well: they were neither slaves nor concubines nor housekeepers nor mere objects of affection or desire. Their life was full on Crete, athletic, artistic, gentle,

and vibrant. Gabrielle was careful to demonstrate that male-
ness was not confirmed by violence, certainly not by violence against women or those weaker than themselves. By
the beginning of Gabrielle's novel, the civilization on Crete
knew that other nations, and particularly Greece, honored
male brutality and cruelty, and sent its men to find their
rewards for war in the rape and carnage and destruction of
other lands.

Years earlier, Crete had demanded as price for passage
through its waters a yearly tribute of youth—seven men and
seven women—to emigrate to Crete and live among its
people. These youths were not sacrifices; they were warmly
welcomed strangers to the life and genetic stock of Crete.
The need for new blood, what we would call a new gene
stock, was known by the rulers of Crete, if not properly
named. Those youths, women and men, the bull leapers
who did their acrobatics on the horns of bulls—the male
symbol of renewal on Crete, the original animal god and
spouse of the queen—developed skills and confidence. They
were not destined for destruction, nor a mindless tribute, as
all the Greek myths recounted.

Now the ancient Cretan culture at the palace of Cnossus
faced destruction from violent Greek forces, to be led by
Theseus. Could Ariadne outwit them? While Emmanuel's
modern plot had depended on but neither admitted nor ex-
pounded its Greek original, Gabrielle's began with the exact
prehistorical moment at which the Greek myth began. Kate
had, meanwhile, glanced at enough of the manuscript to
know that, after its beginnings in those prehistoric times
rediscovered and reconstituted about a century ago by
Evans, the main part of the novel moved to the mid-
twentieth century when Ariadne, now renamed Artemisia,

again waited for the character Emmanuel Foxx had modeled on Theseus.

But at the beginning of Gabrielle's novel, the Cretan Ariadne, aware through her prophetic powers of the imminent destruction of her home and her civilization, consulted Daedalus as her mother had before her. Daedalus wanted no part in the emerging Greek male-centered world. His son, Icarus, had found the possibility of patriarchy and war exhilarating, and Daedalus had had to watch his son, swollen with his new-learned manly pride, fly too near the sun and melt the wax wings he had stolen from his father. Daedalus had known he had stolen them, had known that Icarus, allowed to live, would betray them all. The lesson Ariadne learned from this was that Greek men and their ilk would, in time, destroy themselves, but not perhaps until they had destroyed the whole earth with them.

Daedalus did not have much time to tell Ariadne all he knew. Crete would be conquered; there was no chance of avoiding that. The old ways were gone, women would be enslaved or made into objects of male desire, largely powerless. Other races too, believed to be of less valor and worth than Greeks, would likewise be enslaved. Listening to him, Ariadne despaired.

Daedalus explained that there was no present help, except to let Theseus believe that he had conquered easily, conquered because of Ariadne's lust for him. He would take her and Phaedre away. Phaedre's part would come soon enough; she would cause Theseus to kill his son, the embodiment of masculine self-aggrandizement, thus preventing much suffering and avenging Hippolyta, whose son he also was. Hippolyta, too, would await the future, in spite of any story Greek myth might tell of her.

THE PLAYERS COME AGAIN

Ariadne must pretend lust for Theseus, and allow him to take her away. But once on the ship, she must sufficiently horrify him to force him to put her ashore at Dia, a Cretan island, where Dionysus would come to her rescue and assure her survival and her eventual return. Very eventual, Daedalus said, but certain. Not certain to succeed, but certain to try.

And Ariadne did as he advised. To frighten Theseus and make him desert her, she pretended a frenzy, such as he had heard women were prone to, and pleaded for male flesh to feast upon. Her act was good; so good it frightened even her. He sailed near to the shore at night, carried her onto the island of Dia, and told his crew that he would return for her next day. Next day, he pretended to have forgotten her. The crew, equally horrified at what they had seen, or at what others had described, did not remind Theseus. Was it Ariadne who made him forget to change his black sails to white to tell his father he was returning alive? No, it was not Ariadne, it was Theseus himself, eager to take his father's place, eager to sail under the colors of manhood.

So ended the first part. Kate plunged immediately into the second part, which began again as Emmanuel's novel had begun, with the modern heroine awaiting the arrival of the Theseus figure. Gabrielle's modern heroine, Artemisia, knew that the time for the revival of the Micean civilization had come. Like Joyce's Stephen Dedalus, Artemisia prayed: "Old father, old artificer, stand me now and ever in good stead." She borrowed Joyce's words to say: "Welcome, O life! I go to encounter for the millionth time the reality of experience and to forge in the smithy of my soul the uncreated conscience of my race."

Gabrielle had read Joyce too.

*   *   *

Some days after Kate had returned home, taken up the strands of her former, by now quite strangely unfamiliar, life, answered countless letters, returned time-consuming phone calls, devoted days to restoring some sort of order to her affairs, she settled down to tell Reed all about the decision before her. She had by now reread all of Gabrielle's novel and felt strangely empowered by it. She tried to explain this to Reed.

"I'm probably gaga, a sensation I have become quite used to since encountering Gabrielle and her connections however far-flung. I mean, even Simon Pearlstine seemed like a figure out of nowhere, a visitor from another planet."

"Conclusions first," Reed said. "Explanations and excuses later."

"Conclusions are what I don't have. If I leave out explanations and excuses, all I have left is a question."

"Ask it."

"Ought I to edit this crazy book and write a biographical portrait and what shall I tell Simon?"

"That's three questions. Do you want to edit the book? No, let me ask it differently. What do you think the book is about?"

"I hate people who ask what novels are 'about,' " Kate rather irritably responded.

"What is it about the novel that strikes you as either brilliant or terrifying or ridiculous depending on your mood and state of sobriety?"

"It's so incredibly ahead of its time. It's a book written after all at the height of high modernism, or not long after— we can't really know when she wrote it, except not before

206

the 1920s, when Emmanuel Foxx was working on *Ariadne*, and not after 1955, when Anne visited her and spirited the papers away. My guess is that it was mostly written in the thirties and forties, maybe with time out for the war, maybe not. She may have polished it up in the early fifties in London. What was your question?''

"Kate, you grow wordier and less coherent by the minute, the very second. You are often this way when your cases show signs of reaching a solution which is usually, in the way of solutions, a compromise and unsatisfactory, but I've never known you to babble on like this when it was merely a matter of literature. Sorry: I withdraw the 'merely.' When it was a matter of literature. My question was: what about the novel disturbs you?''

"Good novels are supposed to disturb you. All right, I'll stick to this one, don't go into your prosecuting-attorney act, leaping to your feet to object every time I open my mouth.''

"It isn't just prosecutors who do that," Reed mildly said. "Go on.''

"Look here, as you may have noticed, being a feminist or at least suggesting that patriarchy is not the most divinely perfect scheme ever devised hardly leaves me unassaulted and unridiculed even in these more or less feminist times. It's clear that Gabrielle had no illusions about remaining unattacked at worst, or ignored at best, if she published anything as radical, as revolutionary, as her novel. She might have published it and hoped to be ignored in her lifetime and rediscovered at a later date if she had not been Foxx's wife. As it was, she was sure to be discovered, if only because her novel so clearly took off from his, and

207

maybe she wasn't a watching-the-shit-hit-the-fan type, to put it crudely."

"At least it's clear," Reed acknowledged. "But that was then. Won't the novel be seen now in an altogether different light, won't its importance be obvious? And since you're in no way connected with Gabrielle, what onus can be ascribed to you?"

"I teach literature. This novel attempts to subvert, hell, to show up Emmanuel Foxx's masterpiece, to say nothing of bringing into question the whole masculine bias of high modernism. And by the wife and inspiration of one of the highest of modernists. My God, Reed, it will probably make *People* magazine. I can hear all the critics already. Don't you *see*?"

"I think you ought to present it. Edit it where necessary, write a snappy but elegant account of her life, leaving out the steamy bits, and send it all off. If Simon Pearlstine doesn't want to publish it, somebody will for certain. Give him back his advance, the part you've already received, and Bob's your uncle."

"Do I want to be the center of a maelstrom, an academic and literary debate that will probably go on for years? It will make the question of whether the governess in Henry James's *The Turn of the Screw* was fantasizing look like nothing."

"That is a question I seem to have managed to live a not uneventful life of many years without confronting. I'm the sort who might even not notice Gabrielle's novel if I weren't married to you. All right, I know that's not the point. Are you afraid, Kate? Is that what it comes down to?"

"I'm the retiring type, though you may not have noticed."

"I have noticed. Types who seem retiring usually resemble Uriah Heep. You see, a literary allusion."

"Suppose I don't do it?"

"Get someone else to. I'm sure it would be the making of most on-the-make academic careers."

"I would have to persuade Anne and Dorinda and Nellie."

"No persuasion would be necessary. You have only to persuade yourself. You can *tell* Anne and Dorinda and Nellie. Now tell *me* I'm not being helpful."

"You're being horribly helpful, like a Spartan mother telling her son to come home with his shield or on it."

"I always understood you had no interest in men who told you what you wanted to hear if they didn't agree with it."

"So glad you know what I want to hear; do you mind telling me?"

"You want to hear that you must do this, are under a moral obligation to do it, have no choice."

"And you believe?"

"I believe you have a choice. I think you should estimate the risks and the benefits, and decide on that basis. If you want to be shoved into doing it, let your obvious desire shove you. If you want to be prevented by fear of the brouhaha, don't look for comfort from me. I think there probably will be a wild brouhaha, Gabrielle will be accused of Utopian, ridiculous schemes to undermine the patriarchy, to say nothing of every religion in sight, and you will be seen as an unfeminine, man-devouring, balls-crushing, lesbian, strident, shrill women's libber."

"No one uses that phrase anymore."

"Then they'll reinvent it, or worse. If that all sounds

rather terrifying, which it does, let someone take the rap for whom the academic and media rewards of success and fame will be welcome, even desired."

"But Anne and Dorinda and Nellie . . ."

"I don't even believe they exist, if you want to know the truth." Reed marched into the kitchen to gather the makings of drinks. "Single-malt scotch?" he asked, rattling ice trays.

"They exist."

"Not for the purposes of this decision."

"They trusted me."

"The number of people who have trusted you since we met, and no doubt before, challenge enumeration. That didn't entice you into publishing lost manuscripts and writing truncated biographies. Damn it, Kate, sleep on it. When you wake up you'll know what you want to do. Now, we've kicked it around enough to satisfy anyone's unconscious and conscious scruples. Do you want to hear about my day? Law students are beginning to doubt the value of the Socratic method. The world as I knew it is fast passing away, and a good thing too."

"My governess used to read me a fairy story in which a woman keeps saying: 'Morning is wiser than evening,' " Kate announced.

"I knew your governess would agree with me," Reed said. "We got you at different times of life, but we both knew the right thing to say. Don't worry. You'll know in the morning. Skoal!"

And he raised his glass to hers.

He was right. In the morning Kate called Simon Pearlstine and said that she had to see him immediately. He was booked for lunch, but agreed to meet her for a drink at six at The Stanhope. Kate spent the day girding her loins in a manner she hoped Ariadne and Daedalus would have approved. And Gabrielle.

And Anne and Dorinda and Nellie. Who, Kate decided, she would have to see together and all at once before much more time had passed. Nellie would have to be enticed to New York and away from Geneva as soon as possible.

Simon first.

Eleven

KATE approached The Stanhope warily; it was not the sort of meeting place she preferred; it wanted only the "right" people to occupy its tables and generally indicated that it was conferring rather than receiving a favor while acquiescing in one's presence. Kate disliked cultivating headwaiters for the right to patronize their establishment, but Simon had clearly got the cultivation of maître d's down to a science, for he was there at a ringside seat when she arrived. Rising, and helping her to get seated, he gazed at her with apprehension.

"You look at me as though I were about to pull a rabbit out of my pocketbook," Kate finally said.

"Good description. I was waiting for you to pull out the advance so far paid, in cash. Are you about to do that?"

"You are prepared for a dramatic moment."

"Shouldn't I be?"

"Yes, in a way. Let me tell you what has happened, and then, if that seems proper, I shall gladly return the advance, though not in cash. Sorry not to play the scene with sufficient drama. Actually, though, it's dramatic enough. Scotch and soda," she added, as the waiter hovered. "Small scotch, large soda."

"Two scotch and sodas," Simon told the waiter, naming the brand. "Soda on the side. And may we have something to munch on?"

"Certainly, sir," the man said, as though Simon had caught him out unfairly. Kate thought with a certain pleasure of the café in Geneva where she and Nellie had sat and no one had tried to impress, hurry, or embarrass them. Now, was she being quite fair? Perhaps she was only projecting her own discomfort onto this ambience. All the same, people clearly came here more for a matter of status than pleasure. Kate never believed in forgoing pleasure for any but the most profound reasons, and certainly not for anything as ephemeral and useless as status. . . . Then suddenly, for no discernible reason, she knew it was going to be all right. And after all, why shouldn't Simon have a drink at The Stanhope? He lived around the corner somewhere, and it really was a pleasant place to sit in the late afternoon.

"When you're finished woolgathering," Simon said, "you might put me out of my misery. Just say 'no biography' if that's the horrible message, as I fear it is, and you can explain everything later. Here's your drink. If you have bad news, I can always have another scotch, larger and laced with bicarbonate of soda. Is it 'no biography'?"

"That's right. No biography. But there will be a very exciting book, if you want it. And I can always add on a short biography, more of a portrait really.'' Kate welcomed her drink, added the soda, and sipped it gratefully. "It's rather a long story I'm afraid.''

"I take it Nellie has indeed burned everything, including your intentions regarding her grandmother.''

Who's not her grandmother, Kate thought of saying, but did not. She had determined not to mention to anyone (except Reed) the secrets she had heard. She saw that as part of the bargain. The truth about Nellie's father and even Anne's might come out someday, but it did not seem to her that it was her task to bring those stories into circulation. If she understood the bargain, she would edit Gabrielle's novel, add a (it was to be hoped) well-written, concise biography of Gabrielle, and leave the Foxx and Goddard secrets to silence or, at least, another generation's efforts at detection.

"You remember the papers that Anne took from Gabrielle's room, the ones she put in a vault and, as far as I can tell, forgot about for decades?''

"Of course I remember. I'm the one who sent you Anne's memoir, you do recall that?''

"Simon, please don't be petulant. In fact, be patient. This won't take forever, but I have to tell it in my own way.''

"Patience is my byword, indeed my standard.''

"Glad to hear it. I've always thought patience . . .''

"Kate, if you start on some disquisition on patience, however perceptive, I shall choke you on the spot and The Stanhope will never give me a table on Fifth Avenue again. What happened to Gabrielle's papers after they had languished for decades in some bloody bank?''

"It was a very nice bank.''

"KATE!'' Simon ejaculated, causing those seated at

nearby tables to raise their heads and regard him with a mixture of curiosity and disdain.

"We got the papers from the bank, took them back to a house in Highgate Anne had borrowed, complete with cat. We had a very nice woman taxi driver after we had liberated the papers, but I'll skip that part." Kate smiled at Simon and he ruefully smiled back. "The papers had been bundled together any which way, and it took us the better part of a week to get them into some sort of rational order. Not to keep you in suspense, let me say that they turned out to be a novel written by Gabrielle, really a kind of counter novel to Emmanuel Foxx's *Ariadne*. That we were able to decide which pages went where was wholly due to the fact that she had, in a rough way, structured her novel on Foxx's. It is Gabrielle's version of the Ariadne story, standing in contradiction to Emmanuel's version. Her novel's rather wonderful, if you want to know, and the point of my being here this afternoon and drinking this lovely scotch is to suggest that I edit her novel, and add, if you decide to publish my edition and agree with this idea, a short biographical portrait of Gabrielle that I shall try to make as elegant as possible. And I have brought back my advance, not in cash, I'm afraid, nothing so dramatic. Just a check. I suppose we'll have to write a new contract if you're interested, or else just tear up the old one. I hope you aren't going to be dreary and legal about it, though I admit I've put you in an awkward position."

"Awkward. Just the word of all the possible words I would have chosen."

"I do think, dear Simon, that you, that is to say your publishing house, will do wonderfully well with this novel. My own opinion, for what it's worth, is that it will alter everyone's view of high modernism, it will bring gender to the foreground of what had previously been a rather reactionary and male literary period, and it will get a great deal of attention indeed.''

"I have to take it up at an editorial meeting, needless to say, but of course we'll want it. Why are you giving me back the advance in any form of currency?"

"Because we have to make an entirely new arrangement. The royalties from Gabrielle's novel will go to Nellie and Anne. You can pay me a fair price for my biographical portrait, if you want it, perhaps even a sliver of the royalties for the introduction and the editing, whatever is fair. And I would be grateful if you helped a bit with the expenses of editing: research, typing, copying, that sort of thing. Do we have a deal, always assuming your editorial meeting agrees?"

"You take my breath away. Nor am I sufficiently breathless to ignore the fact that you're sitting on a whole lot of information about Gabrielle you've decided to hold out on. There has to be some reason why you abandon a full-length biography with such alacrity. After all, we could do both the edition of her novel and a book-length biography, no reason not."

"We could," Kate said, "but I don't want to do all that. And with the letters burned, I honestly don't feel there's that much to say. Whatever Gabrielle really was and thought, wherever she had her being apart from her obvious role as Emmanuel's wife, is in her novel. Scholars and biographers will be reconstructing her life from that novel for years to come. Simon, please take the check, order us another drink, and try to find out as soon as possible if your company wants to do Gabrielle's novel my way."

"Kate, no one ever gives back an advance, not without an extended court case or under the most unlikely circumstances. I'm afraid you do need an agent, contrary to my earlier advice. At least hold on to the advance until we know where we are. You did interview people, travel, spend time. Let's not talk about money right now; let's talk about a publication schedule."

"I'll try to do the editing in a year, and the portrait, if you want it, as soon after that as I can. I'm a fast worker."

"So I've noticed. That's a lot of work for a year."

"All right, two years. If we settle this, I'll start right now and keep going until I reach the end. If you want to do this . . ."

"Stop saying 'if.' Of course I want to do it. We ought to be talking money in a more orderly manner. Perhaps I should talk to your lawyer husband. Do get an agent; I'm beginning to feel like a confidence man talking an impoverished widow out of her pittance."

"Naïveté is not my mode," Kate said, "though I have been known to be humble under the proper circumstances. Stop worrying. I want to make sure that Nellie and Anne get the royalties, and if I understand advances, they're only against royalties anyway. You'd have to pay it to them, which seems a bit odd. I realize this is an unusual situation: I have a talent for them. Simon, will you please just decide if you want to do this book or not? I think the fact that Anne sent you her memoir might be looked on as a manifestation of your rightness for this task. Dorinda's network thinks you're sound, really sound."

"When do I get to read the novel, in the form it's in now, the one you've got?"

"When the contract is signed, all agreements made, all

217

that behind us. In other words, given the trouble lawyers can make about any arrangement for the benefit of their billable hours and the assurance that, in the most unlikely events, their client has the upper hand, probably in about six months. But if you think you want to go ahead, I'll get started. After all, I'm going to edit it for someone.''

''That's the perfect exit line,'' Simon said. ''But don't exit. Tell me more about the novel. Tell me more about Nellie and Anne and Dorinda. Have you met Dorinda?''

''I've met them all,'' Kate said. ''They're like a coven of good witches, if you can imagine that. They're all in their sixties, and I keep thinking of them as young women, not in looks but in attitude, manner, vigor. It's as though they only found the point of youth when it stopped oppressing them and let them be young.''

''That's a wonderful Fansler statement, full of profundities that make either no sense or the greatest sense. Well, I do see what you mean. Is that why they, or Anne, suddenly decided to liberate Gabrielle's novel after all this time?''

''They were waiting for the perfect moment in the history of modernism,'' Kate said. ''And do you know, having consulted a number of colleagues on the matter, I think they found it.''

''They were waiting for you,'' Simon said.

''I happened to be on the horizon when they needed an editor,'' Kate said, ''and when I was looking for a new adventure. Just as you were looking for a good book. We both just mistook the exact nature of what we were about.''

The waiter appeared, and Simon ordered another round, omitting the bicarbonate of soda. He looked, Kate thought, like a man who found money on the street and didn't quite know what to do with it. No, he looked like someone who had received a gift and wasn't sure what accepting it would entail. On the whole, Kate decided, smiling at him, he looked pleased.

Indeed, he was. When all the arrangements had been made, remade, refined, redefined, and quibbled over, Kate had the contracts on her desk and realized that she was actually going to have to do the job she had talked herself and Simon into. She had also been talked, if not skillfully manipulated, into it by the three beneficent witches, Dorinda, Anne, and Nellie.

Before she got actively under way in the editing of Gabrielle's manuscript, she intended to have a long talk with the three of them together. For Kate, that alone would be the end of the beginning.

She had summoned (invited was the kinder but rather less accurate word) the three of them to her apartment. Nellie had flown to New York not only for this meeting and a reunion with the rest of the triumvirate but also to sign the contracts for the publication of Gabrielle's novel with Simon Pearlstine's company and with Kate. Nothing, it seemed, was done these days in publishing or anywhere else without contracts spelling out every conceivable and inconceivable eventuality from death to disinclination. The lawyers for Anne and Nellie, recruited by Dorinda, had prescribed the most careful restrictions on the kind of publicity they would countenance for Gabrielle's book, and Kate had, on the advice of yet another lawyer, insisted upon okaying the jacket and catalogue copy.

Bright young people, to judge from Kate's students, still seemed to want to go into publishing despite the fact that it was as underpaid as it was unaesthetic in its aims. She had now decided after this experience to advise them to publish a book instead. One surely learned from that operation more about the perils and mechanics of publishing than by acting as the assistant to someone in subsidiary rights.

All three—Dorinda, Anne, Nellie—agreed to come to Kate's apartment and sip their preferred drinks in her living room. Kate had determined to leave forever as strange and unknown to her as they now were the homes, together with the two eccentric male companions, of the three women. In addition, she wanted to be in charge of this encounter, to stage-manage it, if one were to put it frankly, to learn what she had to learn and go on to the next stage of her life—the editing of Gabrielle's novel—with the past spoken of by them all, however secret, however never to be revealed it would then remain.

The three arrived together, Dorinda chatting as soon as she entered, the others more silent, as she imagined they had been in their girlhood. Anne and Nellie she had come to know fairly well, to admire, to like, to be glad they had chosen her to figure in their lives and plans. Dorinda she knew less well, but had more active affection for. She knew Dorinda's life. However different it had been from Kate's in one or two of its aspects—certainly no one in Kate's family had ever done anything half so interesting as marrying a famous author, or indeed anything interesting at all, except, Kate admitted to herself, making money, which they found interesting and which she was interested in spending in her own way—except for those one or two aspects, Dorinda had lived Kate's life a generation earlier. And Kate knew what a numbing and terrible time that generation of women had endured. Dorinda was beginning to awaken, and if awakening had come rather late in her life, the sudden revelation of what mattered had revealed itself to her and Kate at about the same moment in the course of the twentieth century. Dorinda, like so many vital women, had been full of beans as a girl, had then gone into a dreaming sleep for many years, disguised as sex object, mother, hostess, housewife, and had only now resurrected herself. Kate believed in born-again women, and Dorinda was a rare and wonderful example.

"Beer for Anne," Kate said, sticking as always to the fundamentals, "sherry for Dorinda, and what for Nellie? Or have you all changed your minds?"

"We've brought a bottle of French champagne," Dorinda announced, extracting it from her compendious leather bag. "It's really French," she assured them, as though champagne was in the habit of appearing surreptitiously in other countries. "We thought we might drink to Gabrielle's novel and to you, Kate."

"We can't start with champagne," Kate said, taking the bottle from Dorinda. "Devoted as I am to libations and the lovely rituals of wine and companionship, we've got to have reached certain understandings before I celebrate. I'll put this in the refrigerator to keep it cold for the right moment if it comes. What would you like in the meanwhile?"

"But I thought everything was settled," Dorinda said, flopping onto the couch like a package dropped from an airplane. "Sherry for me, as always. I thought we were celebrating Gabrielle's novel which you are editing, together with biographical portrait. Can't we celebrate that?"

"Not exactly," Kate said. "Anyway, not yet. Beer, Anne?"

"I'm rather off beer since our days at the Hampstead pub," Anne said. "British bitter on draft is not to be followed by bottled anything, at least for a while. Do you have white wine?"

"White wine it is," Kate said, "and I quite agree with you about the bitter on tap; I wish we had some now. And you, Nellie? We only drank coffee in Geneva."

"White wine for me too," Nellie said, sitting on the couch with Dorinda. Anne followed Kate into the kitchen to help with the drinks.

"It's a funny thing and I just noticed it," Anne said as Kate collected bottles and glasses. "When we were young, Dorinda was so much better-looking than I. And now we're old women and there is nothing to choose between us. I suspect that's because neither of us has bothered much with trying to pass for young. Of course, Dorinda is thinner, there is that."

"Slimness is either in the genes, or earned at tremendous cost," Kate said. "I wouldn't give it another thought. You both look wonderful, if you want to know."

"Thank you. That's how we feel; it's quite extraordinary." Kate and Anne returned to the living room and sat in the chairs on either side of the couch.

"No cat, however," Anne said.

"Two minds that move together," Kate said. "I was just thinking that Lavinia's cat ought to be here at this moment. I think of her as a familiar; isn't that what witches called their cats?"

"Are we witches?" Dorinda said. "What fun." Nellie and Anne looked startled.

"Of the very best kind," Kate said, "like the door-mouse's butter. There has been something Alice-in-Wonderland about all this; believing six impossible things before breakfast, having all the wickets move because they're animals, going through mirrors. Perhaps you know what I mean."

"Fathers turning out to be someone else, all except mine," Dorinda said. The others sipped silence with their wine. Dorinda, Kate suddenly understood, was the leader, the one who made it all happen, the one who had always made it all happen. Whoever anyone's father was had nothing to do with it; it was Dorinda who had wanted Anne and then Nellie with her, who had wanted it again sometime in her early fifties, perhaps just after her encounter with Mark Hansford.

"There were rather a lot of secrets," Nellie said. "And burned letters; I know you regret that. But there probably wasn't anything in them that was important. Gabrielle just wanted the record swept clean; I think she wanted to be remembered as herself, by her novel."

"Except," Kate said, looking at Nellie, "you mentioned that I was a detective the first time we met. I am, you know, though only of an amateur and rather literary kind. Did you speak to me about my being a detective because you wanted me to stop being, to restrict my detecting to Gabrielle's manuscript?"

Anne spoke: "Nellie meant that it would take a literary detective to discover the order of Gabrielle's pages. She has certainly been proven right. Besides, aren't all scholars really detectives? Hasn't somebody said so?"

"What brought you three together again, so many years after Gabrielle died?"

"I began reviewing my life," Dorinda said. "That dreadful Mark Hansford was the beginning of that, I can see now. Once I'd broken free from the spell of Arthur, I seemed to gather strength at every turn. I went back to the beginning, to Anne and Nellie. We got back in touch, we began to talk, we rekindled our friendship. Can I have more sherry?"

Kate poured it for her. "And was it when you three began talking again that you decided to do something about Gabrielle's papers?"

"Not right away," Nellie said. "It took us a while to become close again, to begin to talk about the past, about our fathers, all of that."

"Not until Emile died, in fact," Kate said. "That was when it became safe to talk about Gabrielle, and Emile, and all the rest of it. That's when Dorinda told her mother about Nellie, when Eleanor told Dorinda about Anne. Did you tell her the rest of it? Did you trust her not to tell me when I went to see her, or hope that she would tell me?"

"Tell you what?" Dorinda said, without conviction.

"Answer me, please," Kate said. "I want to know if Eleanor knew."

"Yes," Dorinda said, sighing in a fatalistic manner. She exchanged glances with the other two. "My mother knew. She thought we should tell you everything but that. She was used to keeping secrets, you see. But I wanted to give her the chance to see you and decide to tell you if she wanted to. She likes you very much, but she thought that was something no one else had to know; we decided no one would know, ever."

"Are we near to the champagne?" Nellie asked. "I don't want to sound impatient, but I'd like to celebrate Kate's editing and Gabrielle's manuscript and get on, the rest of us, with the rest of our lives. I feel as though Gabrielle were giving us a gentle shove into the future. I'm trying to get a job with the U.N. and move back to New York."

They wanted to leave it all unsaid. But Kate knew that it

had to be said. You cannot ignore bodies: you can only give them proper cremation and scatter the ashes. Ideas are the same.

"Did Gabrielle tell you in London that day you took the papers, or the day before, Anne? Did she tell you she had killed Emmanuel? Or did she tell you the truth, that Emile had killed him? Or did she fail to mention it at all?"

Anne recognized necessity when she met it. "She told me. She said I was not to tell Nellie. She said I was to tell no one, just to put her papers away somewhere safe. She said she told me only so that if anyone should come to suspect Emile, I could testify that it wasn't Emile, it was her."

"So she knew Emile was still alive."

Nellie spoke: "Oh, yes. She was afraid of what Emile would do even before Poppop died. That was why she urged me to go to America. That was why she asked Eleanor to send for me. She didn't tell Eleanor why, but she knew Eleanor would manage it. And as I told you in Geneva, I wanted to go. The atmosphere was poison, even before Emile left to join the Resistance, even before Poppop died."

Kate said: "And you told no one, Anne? You just put the papers in the vault and tried to forget the whole thing?"

"Eventually I told Eleanor. I had to tell someone. I didn't know the right thing to do. Eleanor never blinked an eye. And she helped to pay for the bank vault, which was really a lot of money. She said I should trust Nellie and Dorinda, that they would be my strength. It took me a while, but in the end I followed her advice, which was fine, as always." Anne smiled at the others.

"What made you guess?" Dorinda said. "I thought we

225

gave you so many secrets you wouldn't expect there could possibly be any more.''

"That's the first thing I learned when I set out upon the sticky road of detection: when the fellow is asking you to watch the hat, look for what he isn't asking you to see. That's where the action is. The rabbit isn't in the hat; he's wherever the fellow's other hand is.''

"We would have done better not to have a rabbit.''

"Much better. As a straight literary proposition I would, in all probability, have jumped at it. But, you may notice, I'm still jumping at it. So there isn't much lost after all.''

"I know exactly what you mean," Dorinda said. "Ever since I was a very young child, I couldn't ignore a loose thread sticking out. I had to pull on it until I found whatever was at the end. If no one left a thread out, I might well ignore the whole thing. I should have remembered that before we decided to be clever.''

Kate said: "It's not many families, however extended, who have two children born on the wrong side of the blanket, as they used to say in old English novels, let alone a murder to account for.''

"Poor Emile," Nellie said. "I think when he learned about me—and certainly either Hilda or Emmanuel or both must have told him, or at least made sure he'd guess—it must have been the last straw. His hatred of his father was intense.''

"It's enough to make one tip one's hat to Freud," Kate said, "something I'm not usually likely to do when it comes to the family romance. He's quite good, of course, on repression. Do you think Gabrielle helped Emile?''

"No. I think she probably tried to stop him," Nellie said, "but she couldn't know for sure what he was up to. I'm certain he didn't tell her, not in so many words. I suspect Emile poisoned his father slowly; that was why he seemed ill. Food was short, everything tasted funny, off somehow, we had to eat it however it tasted. But Emile knew he could count on her covering for him. And there was a war, and Emile could go off afterward and be a hero and die. So many people were dying around that time: James Joyce, and Virginia Woolf, thousands of young men, and all kinds of people in the bombings. One more death was just one more sorrow.''

Anne said: "We decided to wait for Emile's death before we even brought up the subject of Gabrielle's papers. We didn't think she would have left anything about Emile there; why would she, when she was so adamant about burning all her letters, burning all the records there were? But that was how Nellie wanted it—to wait for Emile's death, that was what Eleanor advised, and that was what we did.''

Dorinda said: "We thought it impressive that Emile let Nellie know he was alive. We thought that was a kind of restitution. It was a kind of kindness. It was a claiming of Nellie even though she wasn't his.''

"When did you decide to write your memoir?" Kate asked Anne.

"After we three had been talking a long while; oh, after we had all learned the truth about everything. Somehow it made the story as I knew it before, as I knew it up to Gabrielle's death, easier to tell. It wasn't the whole truth, but it was the truth I had lived for most of my life, and I wanted to get it down. Dorinda thought it would help to introduce Gabrielle's when we decided to do that, and of course it did. Writing it was a real blessing for me. It was like a cleansing, the way people are supposed to feel after psychoanalysis or therapy.''

"That's what Virginia Woolf remarked about writing *To the Lighthouse*," Dorinda said. "It doesn't have to be the truth, just your vision of it, written down," she added, looking at Anne.

"We will all have our vision," Nellie said. "If one of us does it, we will all be able to do it. I've never believed in friendships that go on from childhood throughout life, unchanged, any more than I believe in very long unchanging marriages. I only believe in rediscovery and reinventing. I'm not putting this well: the three of us didn't want to remember back to when we were children in order to understand our childhood. We want to think forward together; is there a word for the opposite of remembering? Childhood is an overrated time. I think being fifty allows one to escape from being a child, from all of childhood's terrors. That was when we escaped."

"I'll get the champagne," Kate said. She looked at the three women in their sixties, all simultaneously children and mature women, none caught any longer in the past. For them, as for Gabrielle's novel, it was the future that mattered; more even than that, the present mattered.

"No," Kate said to Anne, who was rising. "Don't help me. I want to get the champagne and present it to you three. We'll drink to the four of us, and to Gabrielle's novel."

She went, leaving the three of them together for the moment, smiling at each other, anticipating.

And what would she, Kate, be anticipating? A new kind of job, a new adventure, bringing Gabrielle back to life, as Gabrielle had brought Ariadne back to life. Emmanuel Foxx had had his triumph. No one would ever know his son had murdered him; no one, probably, would ever doubt his genius. And yet Gabrielle's testimony would remain, questioning his testament, debating it.

Kate felt as though a rare chance had come to her, one of those moments when all of the missed opportunities, the less than perfect literary accomplishments, the administrative defeats and the triumph of small-minded men devoted to the past, might be redeemed. The moment would not last, but she let it have its force. She had told Dorinda that all English literature was the story of second chances. This, then, was her second chance, and Gabrielle's, and Ariadne's.

The tray was heavy with the champagne in an ice bucket and the four tall glasses, but Kate carried it to the three waiting women lightly, as an offering.

ABOUT THE AUTHOR

Amanda Cross is the pseudonym of a New York City university professor, Carolyn Heilbrun. This is the tenth Amanda Cross mystery, following *In the Last Analysis; The James Joyce Murder; Poetic Justice; The Theban Mysteries; The Question of Max; Death in a Tenured Position; Sweet Death, Kind Death; No Word from Winifred;* and *A Trap for Fools.*

Be sure to read the complete collection
of
AMANDA CROSS
mysteries,
from Ballantine Books:

DEATH IN A TENURED POSITION
At a sedate and proper afternoon tea, someone slips a
mickey into Janet's Campari and she's found by the police in a most compromising position—drunk on the
floor in the ladies' room. That's when sophisticated
sleuth Kate Fansler shows up to help her old friend figure out who is after her. But before she does, Janet is
found dead—this time in the men's room.

THE JAMES JOYCE MURDER
What can be more idyllic than a summer in the Berk-
shires, sorting through James Joyce's letters to his publisher? What could be more peaceful than long walks in
the woods with friends old and new? Well, just about
anything. Kate Fansler finds that literary ability and
love of nature are far less vital than supersleuthing skill
when her next-door neighbor is murdered—and all her
houseguests are prime suspects.

NO WORD FROM WINIFRED
It seems that a woman named Winifred is missing. The
honorary niece of renowned British novelist Charlotte
Stanton, Winifred had been, of all things, milking cows
on a New England dairy farm when found by the
young woman who wants to write Charlotte Stanton's
biography. But soon after agreeing to cooperate, Winifred disappears. And the would-be biographer desper-
ately needs Kate's help in finding her.

Also by
AMANDA CROSS:

THE QUESTION OF MAX

When Max—well-bred, utterly snobbish Max—asks Kate Fansler to accompany him (to drive him, yet) to the rocky coast of Maine, where the famous author Cecily Hutchins lived until her recent death, Kate reluctantly agrees. Max is literary executor and wants to have a look at Cecily's papers. But first, a little walk to the ocean. Kate, more courageous than her companion, climbs down the rocks and, to her horror, discovers the drowned body of one of her students. The question of how it ended up in this barren place leads sleuth Kate to several intriguing questions about Cecily Hutchins and her Bloomsbury-like literary circle and finally to the question of Max.

SWEET DEATH, KIND DEATH

Every college has its resident "personality," and Clare College, an exclusive women's institution in New England, is no exception. A renowned historian and a successful novelist, the eccentric Patrice Umphelby was an object both of great admiration and utter disdain—until her death by drowning in the campus lake. The verdict is suicide. But the college president grows suspicious and calls in noted professor/detective Kate Fansler.

A TRAP FOR FOOLS

When the body of Canfield Adams, a professor of Middle Eastern culture, is found on the pavement seven stories below his office window, the police see no evidence of foul play. But university officials know that Adams was not one to have jumped out of a window, and there were numerous people—on campus and off—who would have relished pushing him. If the mystery is not resolved, the school may face a hefty lawsuit from the grieving widow.

AMANDA CROSS

To order by phone, call toll free 1-800-733-3000 and order with your major credit card. To expedite your order, mention interest code "LM-791". To order by mail, use the coupon below.